OUR LIVES ARE FULL OF SPECTRES

BY MELANIE ATKINSON

ISBN: 1-7384459-2-9
ISBN-13: 978-1-7384459-2-9

TABLE OF CONTENTS

WHO WANTS TO BE STINKIN' RICH?

"I need your final answer."

The host's voice is grave, and a thin sheen of sweat is coalescing to droplets on the thick mask of his overly-matte studio makeup. The answer cards bearing the show's logo are creasing between his tense, clamped fingers. His self-tan has a definitive line along the delicate webbing of his fingers. It makes him look like he has been seared on a high heat, but only on one side. It is very distracting. I stare for longer than is necessary or comfortable.

"I'm going to have to press you," he pushes.

Annoyance is starting to crack the thin veneer of his professional demeanour. This is wrong. I know it's wrong, but I'm in too deep and the line that should not be crossed is approaching much faster than I expected. I take a deep breath, hold it until I can hear my heartbeat in my ears and then open my mouth, not entirely sure what is going to come out of it – right answer or wrong answer, like a verbal tossing of a coin.

I tell him my final answer. He stays silent. Watching me. I know it's a tactic to ramp up the tension for the audience in the studio and at home, but it's awful, almost physically painful. I want to shake him until the words come spilling out of him like a burst piñata. Just to make it stop. My stomach tenses, waiting for the other shoe to drop, for his stern mouth to tell me that the police are on their way and they were just holding me, watching the transgressions pile up, to see how far I would go and to charge me accordingly. The sound of Marcus panicking is loud in the otherwise silent studio. I can't call out to him, in front of this audience and next to the host, but I stare hard at him, willing him to look up at me. He does. His glasses slip down his nose and he pushes them up again, a subconscious gesture I have seen him make hundreds of times before. He probably doesn't even realise he is doing it but I still wonder how irritating it must be for your glasses to continually slip down your nose for all time.

No-one else can see Marcus, not because he is shy and unassuming, not because he is a figment of my imagination, but because he is dead. Marcus is the ghost who lives in my flat and who has been assisting me with an amazing con that might just make me a millionaire on national television. It's not the money for Marcus. What would he do with money? All the millions and billions in the world won't help him. He'll still be dead. He'll still be wearing glasses that don't fit and a tragically uncool anorak that rustles like a steam train coming past when he moves, even though the actual item of clothing is probably festering in a landfill somewhere, the cheap plastic fabric taking thousands of years to decompose. Money means nothing to Marcus. He's doing it for the love of the competition. That, and peer pressure. My peer pressure.

Marcus was already in situ when I moved in last year. I move a lot. Every place I have lived in has had a ghost, and the majority of them make really annoying roommates who have no intention, or maybe even the ability to ever leave. As roommates go, Marcus is by far the least annoying one I have had. He knows he is dead, for one; some ask you incessantly what has happened and doesn't believe you when you explain that they are no longer alive. Neither does he wail about the fact he is dead, all night and all day like some of the ghosts I have lived with. You wouldn't believe the racket I've had to put up with in the past.

In life, Marcus was a pub quiz champion, something I found out when watching game shows in the flat. Without fail, Marcus would shout the answers to the questions, and he was pretty much always right. I used to leave the game show channel on for him when I went to work. That is when he went from a pub quiz champion to an absolute savant. Every Thursday night we watched *Who Wants To Be Stinkin' Rich?* Together and every week he got nearly every answer correct. It was a stupid throw away comment – *If we went on this show together, we'd easily win!* – that appealed to Marcus's love of games and my two loves of having readily disposable income and also not having to work.

As it turns out, it's a lot different answering questions in the studio, feeling the sweat on the backs of your knees and saturating your pits, rather than being slumped on a sofa at home with crisp crumbs decorating your chest like salty dandruff.

"What song spent the most weeks at number one in 2009?" the host asks.

We're part way in. The cash pot is reasonably healthy and I'm starting to sweat a little less. From his position beside the host, right in my eyeline, Marcus looks at me blankly. Usually he is spitting the answer at me before the host has even finished asking the question. It seems modern music has him flummoxed. I stare at him, willing an answer from his thin lips, but he only shrugs at me.

"How would I know that? I died in 1983! The hit at the time was *Karma Chameleon*!" He mutters. "You don't ever have the radio on. Do you even own a radio? I can't remember the last time I heard the radio."

His face is taking on the glazed look he gets when he is about to become distracted by something else, maybe musing over the decline in wireless radios, or the history of *Culture Club*. I need to keep him focused. Scrunching my eyes up like I'm deep in concentration, I click my fingers a couple of times, hoping it will knock Marcus out of his spiral. It doesn't. He isn't looking at me and I can hear him muttering about Boy George as he stares at his feet.

"Boy," I say loudly, "It's times like these I really wish I could see your cards!"

Chuckling self-deprecatingly, I look over to Marcus, hoping he has understood my hint. Bingo. He nods and looks over the host's shoulder at the cards, which presumably have the correct answers on. His lips move as he reads.

"I GOTTA FEELING!" Marcus yells over to me excitedly, even though I am, hopefully, the only person who can hear him in this room.

We carry on this way for a while, alternating between answers that Marcus knows straight off the bat and a few peaks over the host's shoulder for those that he doesn't. I even know a couple of them. Maybe that is a happy side-effect of watching so many shows with my deceased egghead flat-mate. There is one dicey moment when neither of us knows the answer and the host's thumb is covering it on the card. A particularly dramatic bout of fake crying leads the host to come over to comfort me, putting his arm around me. It does the trick. His hand moves on the card and finally Marcus can see the answer.

Finally, we're at the last answer. Marcus's hand flutters against his anorak. It sounds like the nails of a small animal as it tries to escape a snare. The studio is silent, as though the entire audience are collectively holding their breath. Waiting.

"We should stop," Marcus whispers in my ear.

Shaking my head, I try to wave away his small voice, like an angel on my shoulder, or the embodiment of my conscience. Of course I know it's wrong. I know it is, but the temptation is so strong. If only I could explain to him that it would mean a bigger flat, a nicer sofa, an enormous TV for him to watch his quizzes on, maybe that would tip the balance, maybe then he would agree. Or maybe, even dead, he is a much better person than I.

"This is wrong," he says. I bat at him, making it seem like a fly is buzzing around my face, entranced by my sweaty hairline.

"Yes. That is my final answer." I say over the top of Marcus's protestations.

"YOU'VE JUST BECOME STINKIN' RICH!" the host bellows, making me jump.

Out of the corner of my eye, I can see that his violent expulsion has made Marcus jump too. Before I can say anything at all, the host has gathered me up in his arms, hopping up and down with me in his grip like I've just scored the winning goal in the Cup final. The thin fabric of his shirt presses against my face, and I feel his chest hair grating against my cheek as he bounces. It feels almost obscene, far too intimate a display for a man that I only shook hands with for the first time an hour ago backstage. My face has that thought all over it when he pulls away and spins me to face the audience. I know this because the moment has been immortalised on tape. I saw it on the night it aired, on the re-run and on the copy I set to record. It is only there for a couple of seconds before my hands come up to cover my face, but I've seen it more times than I want to. Marcus asks at least once a month to watch it again. Sometimes I agree but only, I chastise him, on the eighty-inch television in the downstairs recreation room, not in the private cinema. I can't bear to see that expression on the floor to ceiling, surround sound IMAX inspired screen.

MEET ME ON GOOGLE MAPS

I know it's not healthy and I know no good can come of it but the thought never leaves me alone. Ever since those two police officers came to my door, ashen-faced and uncomfortable, it has plagued me endlessly. His last journey. Lying in bed at night, I wonder about it. In my head, I see him get behind the wheel of his car, fiddling with the radio and the heater in the car park of his office. I see him pulling out onto the main road, his hands gently tapping the wheel in time with his music. I listen to his Spotify playlists on repeat and wonder at every song whether it was the one he was listening to when the other car pulled out, too fast, not seeing him until it was too late. Could he hear it over the squeal of metal, the shattering of glass? Was it still playing when they cut him out of the wreckage? Was it the last thing he ever heard?

His face and his mannerisms are all so clear In my mind. We'd driven together enough times that I can conjure him at a moment's notice at the wheel. But I don't know what his last journey looked like. Did he drive past a school and think about future fatherhood? Past a park and think about lazy summer days, walking arm in arm with me? I have to know because if I don't, the last image my brain will conjure will be the last one, and I can't bear to imagine it. The thoughts will not be shaken loose. They take hold, like a vine, creeping into my mind at every opportunity.

Unwilling to waste another entire night lying in my bed, unable to sleep, watching the torturous images my mind has conjured and full of unanswerable questions – Did he cry out for me? Did he know what was happening? – I get up and go downstairs. Booting up my laptop, I open Google Maps and key in the address of his office. I click directions and leave 'your location' as the start point. I add in a stop – the location of the crash, the place he died. The final stop. I let the site calculate the distance. It's five miles from our house to his office. He was only two miles from home when it happened. Two measly miles.

Picking up the little icon for the street view function, I dangle it over the start point, before dropping it into the street below. It's his office. The sight of it is familiar. I'd been to several Christmas parties there. I picked him up from there once, on a frosty December afternoon because he thought he might have appendicitis and didn't want to drive himself to the hospital. His telephone call to come had filled me with panic.

The street view picture is gloriously sunny and blurry-faced people walk past the camera, going about their business. Swinging the viewer round to look at the building, I wonder if he was up there in his office when this picture was taken, talking on the phone, eating lunch at his desk or laughing with a colleague. In that sunny past time he was alive and well, even if he wasn't there. I swing the viewer away and double click the mouse down the road.

I lose the rest of the night as I travel down the route that he would have driven. Bleary-eyed from lack of sleep, I zoom in on the shops he travelled past, opening up a new browser to google them and see what they sold, what other people thought of them from their reviews. I travel around a sunny park, with a blurry-faced woman walking with a stroller, a blurry-faced man walking a dog. I take a traipse round that park of the past and try to imagine the sun on the back of my neck, the call of birds and children, anything that will drown out the screech of metal, the sharp call of his surprise, the rhythmic ticking of his blinker, the blare of his horn cutting through the stunned and abrupt silence. It's a sound that shatters me. It wakes me up in the darkest part of the night, it takes me aback when I'm paying for groceries or texting my boss that *No, I am not ready to return to work just yet.* I don't hear that noise in this park from the past. For a few moments at least, there is relief.

Reluctantly I leave its leafy confines and dawdle for the last few hundred metres of our journey, not wanting to reach the place where I am told the accident happened. I haven't been down that road yet. Only to the corner shop for essentials. Not that I'm ever hungry. Everything tastes like dust in my mouth.

It's getting light out. I could go back to bed and try to get a couple of hours of broken sleep. There is no rule to say that I have to complete this electronic journey. I could just close the laptop and leave it be. I could. But I can't. The urge to see, to know, moves the cursor further along the road. In the middle of the junction is his car. The hand over my mouth does nothing to muffle the scream I make at seeing his car. It lies on its roof, crumpled and decorated with scattered glass, like confetti at a wedding. Several passers-by, their own hands over their own shocked mouths, stand around the scene. Their faces are blurred, like all the others I have seen on this journey, but their shock is palpable. I can feel it through the screen like a heat. The screen shimmers with it. There is a smear of blood on the tarmac, glistening under the afternoon sun of the past. I zoom in desperately to the car's window but he is not there. In the corner of the frame is another person, but their entire body is blurred out, not just their face, like a smudge from a greasy finger on the screen or a tear smearing my vision. I rub my finger over the screen but it is still there, an unclear form with a gossamer thin outline. I can see delicate tendrils of light permeating through. *Is that you? It can't be you!* Grief has muddled me, hallucinated this scene on the screen. I refuse to believe that it is real, that you are just there, on the other side of the pixelated divide. On the other side of the veil.

It might be light outside, but it is still far too early for my sister to receive my frantic, tear-stained phone call. It takes me a long time to explain what I have seen on the computer, and her even longer to understand. Her words are calm and slow, if a little groggy from sleep, as she tries to soothe me, but I can not be soothed. I can only stare at you at the corner of the screen. You're not there when I move the viewer around. Coyly, you can only peek around the corner of a single scene. Her dulcet tones start to wane when I won't be convinced that she can not see the same thing on her phone app. There is more than a touch of annoyance in her voice as she gets out of her nice warm bed to turn on her own computer when I insist she must view the exact location on her own laptop. She sends me screen shots from her phone and from her computer. The scene is not the same. It is an ordinary junction, with a few cars and people walking past. Finally, she pries out of me that I have been up all night and convinces me to close the screen, to get a couple of hours of rest. She says that everything will feel better after some sleep. I don't think anything will feel better ever again.

As I lie in my bed the image from the screen projects onto the back of my eyelids. A cinema of grief. I can't forget it and there is no way that I can sleep. Heaving my exhausted body out of bed, I make my way downstairs. In the brief time I have been lying there, willing sleep to come, the laptop has run out of charge. An intransigent black screen faces me as I hammer on the enter key. Everything is dead. The computer. You. It takes what feels like an inordinately long time to gather enough charge to finally turn back on again. There is a little blinking red light of acquiescence on the computer's side before the screen comes back to life. It opens on the same place, the same junction, but the image is different. Your car is still on its back, like a prone beetle, but now there is an ambulance and a police car in attendance. On the kerb a man is being interviewed by the police, his head in his hands. Is that the man that killed you? The blur is no longer on the edge of the screen and panic jumps into the back of my throat. I can't lose you again. My eyes dart around the until I finally find the smudge, at the back, behind the prone car on the pavement. The breath I have been holding, whooshes out of me with a stifled sob. The smudge is next to a lamppost, on which and old dry bouquet of long-dead flowers is tied. An offering from an earlier bereavement. There is police cordon tape around the scene, and I swear it is fluttering, gently swaying in the summer breeze.

Today the image of you is more defined. It is a little bit easier to convince myself of its reality. There is the outline of your head, your broad sloping shoulders and long legs. You were so tall that you had the tendency to hunch, to make yourself just that little bit smaller. It used to drive your mother mad. It always made me sad. I didn't want you to make yourself less. Maybe because you were everything to me. Larger than life is a cliché, but it feels true. The house is not right without you. Empty. Quiet. If only I could reach through the screen to you. Maybe I could pull you back through. I know that is an utterly crazy thought, but your presence there, your closeness is some comfort. I leave you up on the screen as I go about my day, peeking in on you from time to time from the other room. When the sun sets, I take the laptop upstairs with me, settle it on the pillow next to me. Your pillow. And for the first time since it happened, I fall asleep easily.

When I wake in the morning and boot the computer out of sleep mode, you are not there. The image is the one from my sister's screenshot. Ordinary. Mundane. Everyday. I don't want to see the scene of your accident, but I am desperate to see you again. I load the page a hundred times. I cry in great, wracking sobs. It is like losing you all over again. The image stays the same all day. Resolute. Uncompromising. I go to bed that night without you, to toss and turn and be awakened by the sound that I have conjured up – screeching, crumpling, screaming.

In the morning, without brushing my hair or my teeth, and dressed in the same clothes I have worn for the last week, I leave the house. The sun is dazzling. I've been living with the shades drawn, the only illumination coming from the computer. I am used to the sickly, artificial light of its screen. This sunlight is too bright, too real. I go back into the house to find some sunglasses. In the Autumn sun, they make me look like a starlet who has fallen from grace, hiding from infamy and an inevitable intervention before rehab admission. But they create a barrier between me and the too-real world.

It has been a while since I ate anything of substance and the walk takes me longer than I expect. I feel dizzy and out of place. Out of time. Despite this I recognise the junction as soon as it comes into view. The images on

Google Maps were taken in the middle of summer. Now the trees are wearing their autumn leaves, replete in russet and amber and gold, but it is definitely the right place. Drivers pull in and out, turning and giving way – on their way to drop off their kids at school or go to work. Ordinary. Mundane. Everyday. I don't know if they notice me, scruffy, unkempt and unmoving from the last place on earth I want to be. The bouquet of flowers still clings to the lamppost. The dry and crispy blooms are hanging on by a piece of tightly wound twine. There is a card but I can't read the writing. Too many downpours and morning dews have smudged the words beyond recognition. You are not here. The lamppost flowers make me desperately sad. I wonder whose loved one also lost their life here and why they haven't returned to place another, fresher bunch in place of this one. I wonder if the two of you are together in the after.

There is a petrol station across the road. Outside, next to the lurid newspaper headlines in their plastic boxes, are a couple of buckets of brightly coloured blooms for sale. Still wet from their morning dowsing. I pick the freshest, most colourful looking bunch and go inside to pay.

It takes me a little while to wrangle the old flowers out of their twine, and manoeuvre the new flowers into their place, but it looks good once the job is done. I stand still and watch the breeze move their petals, thinking about you. My fingers are starting to get cold. I'm not dressed for the change in season. It crept up on me while I lay in the cocoon of our bed. By no means have I emerged a butterfly, but maybe I have managed to banish the fear of this road. It is just a road, and I feel a little lighter as I walk home. Maybe I have taken a first step in moving on.

It is several days before I check the page again, expecting to see the standard image, the one everyone else can see. The image on the screen knocks all the breath from my body. You are there. Wearing the suit you wore to work that day. Whole. Not a scratch on you. No totalled car, no police tape, no ambulance, no distraught onlookers to be seen. Your face is not blurry and you are smiling. In your right hand you clutch the bright blooms I left for you that day.

THE HUNTER AND THE HUNTED

"This is it!" Jack bellowed, throwing his arms in the air, a triumphant grin on his face, like a revivalist minister witnessing the first member of their congregation speaking in tongues.

The rest of the team looked less than impressed with the discovery. Behind the overgrown foliage and padlocked gates was the decaying visage of what had once probably been a very handsome building, but was now the rapidly aging former starlet of the property world, sagging jowls and pouched eye bags, crumbling to dust before the mirror of time.

"It's a dump," said Pete, putting words to the expressions of his colleagues.

The heat of anger rubbing under Jack's collar, spreading heat across his chest. He knew it was a dump, but they had to do something to aid their flagging ratings. Only last week they had sat in a loose semi-circle in their makeshift office in Pete's spare bedroom and listened to the television executive on speakerphone.

"The ratings are down boys, I don't know what to

tell you. It's the same across all of our reality TV programming. I guess people want a bit more escapism and a bit less reality these days," he said with faux sympathy. "You've got the next series locked in but then we're going to have to look at the renewal details closely."

Jack had swallowed audibly and asked the question they had all been afraid to.

"Do you mean if the ratings stay down this season, then we might get cancelled?" he'd asked, trying to sound more confident than he felt.

The executive had taken a long time to reply and had punctuated it with a nervous cough before confirming Jack's fears. Jack's stomach sank. He had invested everything into this show and he'd taken it for granted that it would continue until he'd decided he wanted to do something else.

After the executive's answer, Jack had tried to wrap the phone call up as quickly as possible, there was no point in over-egging the pudding of their failure. His failure. The show had, after all, been his idea, his brainchild and his sole focus for the last few years. He had put everything on the back burner, his friendships, his relationship with his partner and his family. Instead of spending time with them he had spent it with his crew, dedicating evenings, weekends and holidays to getting the show off the ground.

The show had started online. They had pooled their resources to buy the expensive equipment, broken into abandoned buildings and spent all night running around inside trying to commune with spirits. They had also taught themselves how to record, edit and upload the footage into something resembling a complete show and done everything they could to cultivate a following. Jack had stayed up night after night chatting with fans and dropping links to the shows until they had a decent sized following. It had all paid off, or so he thought, when the show had caught the attention of a television network looking for more reality TV to add to their roster. For the network the format was relatively cheap. They did not have to pay for sets or actors or writers, just the three guys who had made it their life's work to bring 'Ghost Bros' to fruition.

Their ghost hunting TV show had been popular to start with, high ratings and even, to Jack's immense pleasure, getting recognised in the street. But as the seasons had gone on the interest had waned and along with it their ratings. Jack could sense the end approaching, looming like a spectre behind him. Which was ironic, since the show had never even produced a ghost for their once hungry audience. Jack didn't know what he would do with himself if the end was really nigh. He had a strong suspicion that it might be the death knell of his relationship. He had pleaded and cajoled his partner, telling them that if he just had a little more time, if they could just hold on a little bit longer and stick by him, then it would all be worth it. How could he tell them that it hadn't been worth it? That he was going to have to start again. More late nights and missed dinners and funnelling his money into another scheme that might turn out just like this one. The thought of it dried all the saliva in Jack's mouth. He had to come up with something to pump some life back into 'Ghost Bros'.

The house behind the gates had a history. From his frantic googling he'd been assured it was as haunted as they come, enduring the tragic demise of owner after owner and eventually being boarded up and left to crumble when no-one else wanted to take it on. A sign next to the rusty padlock had once screamed – 'Danger! Keep out!' – but its faded red letters were now more of a whisper. It seemed perfect. They'd advertise it as their most extreme episode yet but with enough nostalgia, brought on by their breaking into the building, to appeal to their long-term, die-hard audience members who had been with them since the show had been internet shorts. Anyway, Jack didn't have the time to try and find whatever solicitor looked after the probate and convince them to let him enter, even if it was for only one night.

Jack had wanted it to be a surprise to the rest of the crew, hoping to film their honest reactions when they got to the site. He hadn't expected those disappointed words from Pete's mouth, assuming his colleague would play his usual role as part of their expeditions – wide-eyed and enthusiastic about the results they could glean from the building they were about to spend the night in. Maybe fame had gone to Pete's head. Maybe he was just tired. None of them were getting any younger and the all-nighters were starting to take their toll. It now took Jack a few days to stop walking around like a re-animated corpse after sleeping away almost the entirety of the next day following a shoot. It used to be that he would leave the shoot, slug an energy drink and go to his day job. Already he was stifling a yawn, even after catching a quick disco nap that afternoon.

Cutting the cameras, so they didn't record themselves committing a crime (or struggling to do so,) Jack, Pete and Harry discussed how they were going to jump the fence.

"Give me a boost", Jack said with bravado that he didn't really feel.

Pete grimaced as Jack's grubby boot stepped into his clasped hands and Jack wondered whether it was that disdain that made him boost Jack a little more enthusiastically than he might have done otherwise. He scrabbled over the fence and just got his legs back underneath him for an ungainly landing on the other side. The two men passed over their bags of equipment –

expensive cameras with night vision capabilities, EMP meters, EVP recorders, spirit boxes, lights and sound recorders so sensitive that they could hear a mouse fart. Jack shuddered to think how much money was in the duffel bags he was carefully placing on the ground. At least if he were desperate, he could sell it to other intrepid ghost hunters. Admittedly it would probably be for a fraction of the price but if the network cancelled the show Jack would be desperate enough. They'd recently moved into a larger house and the mortgage really was extravagant.

Once all three men had cleared the fence, Jack rolled his shoulders, trying to get back into his hosting character, hoping that the worry wouldn't show in his eyes or by the bags under them. They set the cameras rolling again. The night vision camera caught every small bug and speck of dust that flew past the lens as they made their way up to the porch which, it was obvious to everyone even in the low light, was severely rotten. Jack tested the first step with his boot and felt how spongy the structure was, like stepping onto a bouncy castle. They'd be lucky to even make it to the front door at this point, let alone be able to explore the structure. Jack swore, casting haunted eyes at the blinking red light of Pete's camera. They could fix that in editing.

Taking a deep breath, he put one foot onto the porch, hearing the wood complain loudly in the quiet night. After a cacophony of groans, it seemed that the floor of the porch was holding. Jack let out the breath he had been holding and stepped forward again. The board beneath his foot bowed ominously, making him stumble to keep his footing, but it too held. One more step and he was at the front door. He couldn't tell if the door was locked or not, it was far too swollen within its frame. Jack aimed for a spot just below the knob and gave it one sharp kick. The door moved out of place with a wet smack, like a rotten tooth yanked free from an inflamed gum. The stench of the inside of the house hit Jack in the face like a puff of bad breath. It smelt like mould, dust, mouse droppings and as though more than a few of those mice were currently rotting under the floorboards. It smelt like failure.

Unperturbed, Jack stepped through the front door into the cavernous foyer, aiming for the main staircase to the first floor. He didn't hear the floorboards crack. He did however did feel the whoosh of foetid air as he fell through them, past the rot and the woodworm to land with a sickening crack on the concrete floor of the basement. The landing knocked all the wind from Jack's body and the last thing he saw before closing his eyes was the crazed shafts of lights from his crew's torches as they tried to locate him.

When Jack opened his eyes again it was dark apart from a halo of light seeping through the gaping hole that had swallowed him. Where was his crew? Why was no-one helping him? Jack flexed his fingers, waiting for a surge of pain. None came. He flexed his toes. Those too seemed to be obeying his commands with no pain. Jack rolled experimentally to his side before getting his hands under him and pushing himself onto all fours. Mercifully, nothing seemed to be broken. In fact, he felt very little. The absence of pain was almost scarier than if he had broken his arm or leg. The floor beneath his hands was suspiciously sticky. Swiping his finger into the puddle, Jack moved to one of the cracked basement windows and looked at his hand under the soft light of the moon. His fingers were dark with blood. Trying not to panic Jack patted at his body, exploring the unbroken line of his spine, his face and the backs of each leg. As he continued his examination, his fingers probing at the back of his skull, Jack found the source of the blood.

The back of Jack's head and neck were sticky with blood. Under his short hair he could feel the shape of his skull. Panic burbled in his belly. The back of his skull felt caved in, like the delicate shell of a dropped egg leaking precious albumin from its cracked form. Jack continued his investigation, walking his fingers along the ruined surface of his head until he came to a gouge. The force of his impact on the flour had created a lip in his scalp, a deep groove, tacky with blood. Jack's eyes leaked silent tears as his trembling fingers found their way into the gap. He began to retch when his fingertips alighted on the hard surface of bone. What was happening? Why could he not feel any of this? He'd had his fingers inside himself for God's sake, shouldn't that hurt? Shock. He must be in shock, he thought. He'd sustained a terrible injury and adrenaline and shock were keeping him on his feet. He needed to get to a hospital as soon as possible. But where were his crew? Surely they must have seen him fall? Why weren't they down here helping him?

"Hello?" Jack called plaintively through the hole his descent had made in the overhead floorboards.

No response.

Fumbling in the dark, Jack eventually located the staircase from the basement up into the rest of the house. Around the hole he had crashed through was a cordon of blue and white police tape. Jack looked down into the cavernous pit, the depth making him vertiginous. Below him was the cracked-egg silhouette of his own body, looking back up at him with sightless eyes. Jack moaned, deep in the back of his throat, hoping it was a terrible dream or that his crew had decided prank shows would be more profitable and were using him as the first guinea pig in the new pilot.

With that thought, Jack began wildly swivelling his head back and forth, looking for his crew, waiting for them to walk out of the darkness, pointing their fingers and laughing. Eventually his eyes alighted on the two men. But they were not laughing. Pete was looking down at his phone, Harry peering over his shoulder. Both men were staring intently at whatever was on the screen. As Jack came up behind them, he too could see what they were looking at. On Pete's screen was the dark image of Jack from behind, walking into the house before disappearing from view with a scream and the cracking of rotten floorboards. The camera panned down to Jack's staring face, exactly as he'd just seen it.

"I don't think you should," Harry said.

"He'll never believe me. Look, the police have our cameras. I'm going to send it," Pete answered.

Jack watched Pete upload the video into a WhatsApp conversation and press send. The last moments of Jack's life shared with God-knows-who like a TikTok of an amusing cat. Jack shouted and ranted and raved, shouting in each man's face but to no avail. He was a ghost now and his idiot 'ghost hunter' friends had no idea. Jack watched as the police gave them permission to leave, and they exited the gates that had been opened by the emergency personnel. He watched as the police left and finally as the coroner took his broken body out of the building, the paramedics being careful to skirt the obvious patches of rotten floorboards. They were much easier to see under the lights set up by the emergency services. Jack bristled. They had been virtually impossible to see in the dead of night under the eerie green glow of night vision cameras. It wasn't his fault. He wasn't stupid.

Soon he was alone in the pitch black. The cold wind whistled under the front door and fluttered the tape around the hole, whisking errant leaves across the wooden floors. Jack moved around the house, through room after room, peering through rotten scraps of curtain into the gathering grey light of morning. He made it all the way to the third floor, moving across the yawning gaps of stairway with no issue. He was utterly alone. There was no-one else here. None of the ghosts of his research haunted the halls or corridors of this dilapidated mansion. There were no ghosts, no spirits, no entities, no demons or phantoms or spectres. None. Other than Jack himself.

Of course Jack had been sceptical at times, had wondered about the validity of what he and his friends had dedicated their lives to doing. But that hadn't mattered. His whole life had become about the newest bit of kit, the next haunted house or hospital or asylum and above all of that the ratings. More than ghosts, Jack had spent the last years of his life chasing ratings. He checked the stats and the ratings and the reviews and the opinions of his audience online. He had missed anniversary dinners and forgone holidays with his partner to chase the high of increasing ratings. And for what? To die in his thirties and to probably be turned into a cheap internet meme. If he'd still been able to, Jack would have cried, but he seemed to have lost the ability. The inability made him angry. The unfairness of his situation made him angry. His crew's apparent lack of sadness over his demise made him angry. The waste of his life made him angriest of all.

There was no way to release all that fury. No-one to talk to, nowhere to go, just the same four walls to pace around and rage against. Jack felt as though he were going insane with it all. The walls shook with the force of his anger, tiles shimmied from the roof, dust cascaded from the old plaster ceilings, the floorboards jumped and rattled in their grooves. He didn't know how long he had been in the house, how many sunsets and sunrises he had seen and then forgone to shout into the rafters instead. He gave up watching the moon rising in the sky or the stars blinking in the rich velvet of the night. All he did was rage.

It took him a while to realise that there were people outside. He had not been able to hear their approach over the din of his own ire. But the harsh screech of the stiff iron gate, complaining under the weight of a person climbing it, broke through, drawing him to the window. Looking outside, he was confused to see delicate buds swaying in the spring breeze. The sun was setting, a golden orb that bleached the sky around it orange and pink. The season had changed without him realising. How long had he been trapped in this house? Two figures stood inside the gates which had been fitted with new padlocks after the previous ones had been cut away by the emergency services. Even with the light behind them, casting their faces in shade, Jack still knew those figures. He had followed them through dark buildings, he had drunk with them in busy bars, one he had even stood beside at his wedding. Pete and Harry.

If he could have flown out, run them down like an avenging wraith, he would have done. But Jack was bound to the house and had to wait for his erstwhile colleagues to come to him. The mice living in the walls sensed his building anger, like the start of a thunderstorm, and scurried away to safety. The spiders dangling from their webs hastily crawled up their silks to shelter in the rafters. Jack paced the rotten floorboards of the foyer to await his former best friends.

The two men entered the house bathed in the last vestiges of the day's light. They skirted around the hole in the floorboards that had never been fixed and stood in the main foyer, looking around the space. They had no idea that right in front of them Jack screamed and raved and raged. They could not hear him.

"I don't know about this," Harry loudly whispered

to Pete as they carried in their equipment. "It doesn't feel, like, very respectful, does it?" he said to Pete's incredulous face.

"Look I know we weren't expecting that footage to leak and for it to go viral," said Pete contritely, "but it did and now the ratings are through the roof. The producers told me what the numbers were on the re-runs at the weekend and they're better than we were getting on the new episodes back in the day. So, we'd be stupid to lose this momentum mate. I know Jack would understand," Pete said sombrely.

Jack did not in fact understand. Neither did he believe his friend's protestations or apparent contrition. He was pretty positive Pete had leaked the footage of Jack's fall through the floor to bolster their ratings and evidently they were back to capitalise on that momentum. Jack knew he'd been a slave to the ratings but he liked to think if something similar had happened to one of the boys then he wouldn't use their death for clout. Something niggled at the back of his mind while he thought this, but incredulity and anger chased it away to the dark chasms of Jack's conscience.

"What about Louise?" Harry asked.

Jack's stomach fell at the mention of his partner. His insides twisted at the thought of the pain she must be in at his passing.

"Between you, me and the wall," Pete said, gesturing at the mildewy walls with a thumb that barely missed Jack's ghostly eyeball, "she's going to be just fine. If you know what I mean," he continued, waggling his eyebrows suggestively.

Whatever passed for breath caught in Jack's throat. He could taste every mildewy piece of fabric, every clump of dust on the back of his tongue as he struggled to breathe. Not only was this piece of shit using his death for ratings but it seemed like he had moved into Jack's bed too, taking over his life wholesale. Jack's scream was so loud, so forceful that it shut the heavy front door behind the two men, making them both jump.

"Let's just get on with it. This place is giving me the creeps," Harry said while unloading their supplies in the front foyer.

The two men set up a couple of high wattage lamps around the hole and the grim stain on the concrete floor below. They also strategically placed sound recording equipment, an EMF meter and spirit box on the floor. Jack watched them, his fingers twitching with the urge to correct their work. When they flipped the switches on the lights the small space was illuminated with what felt like to Jack the force of a thousand suns. It was as though he was getting the world's worst sunburn, a roasting at the molecular level that was crisping up his cells like a piece of leftover pizza in an air fryer. Involuntarily Jack groaned. The spirit box on the floor jumped into life, crackling with static and the tail end of Jack's moan. All the men in the room, including Jack, stared at the little handheld radio.

"It works," Jack and Pete said at the same time, Jack incredulously, Pete merely confirming that the equipment was actually turned on.

The fact that the equipment had actually worked, had actually heard him, gave Jack an idea. For the next several hours he led the two men in a game of cat and mouse around the dilapidated house. He called to them from the mildewy master bedroom, knocked on pipes in a guest ensuite bathroom and stamped his feet on the old, cracked tiles of the galley kitchen. He heard the crackling feedback of his words, snatches of vowels and consonants in the computer's mechanical voice. The boys were soon run ragged, overexcited by the footage they were getting but out of breath from the constant trips up and down the rickety staircases.

Just before dawn, when the hint of the sun was causing the world to become monochrome, Jack led the two boys into the library. On the top of a bookcase a wood pigeon gently cooed from its nest of stolen words. Jack now knew every inch of this house, which parts were sturdy and which parts were almost entirely rotten. The library's floors were particularly bad and anyone could see that if they really looked. But to the casual onlooker, the boards were covered by musty moth-eaten rugs and looked sturdy enough. You would have to regard the floor carefully from the door to see the way it sagged in the middle, as though even the threadbare rugs were too heavy for it. Jack had done just that – he had examined and analysed every inch of this house since it had taken his life. The boys had not. They had never got this far the first time they had entered it and now they were too excited by the golden evidence they had been capturing of Jack all night. They did not think or even pause before walking out into the middle of the room.

Jack had stopped moaning and groaning. He prowled the edges of the room, waiting to lure the men forward. The house was silent apart from the various foundational creaks and the light scurrying of its many animal residents. It was so quiet that the sound of the floorboards bowing and cracking was like that of a great tree falling, thunderous and deafening, amplified ten-fold through the sensitive earphones of the ghost hunters' equipment. They not only heard but felt as the floor of the once opulent room finally gave way, crashing down through the floors below and subsequently into the basement of the house. Jack watched the whole thing, as both men disappeared in a hail of dust and wood and plaster and screaming. He felt the house rattle as the debris struck the first floor, heard the sickening creak as those boards also gave up their tenuous hold and finally crashed into the concrete basement where he had met his own demise.

His ears rang after the cataclysmic noise of the middle of the house shearing away from the edges of itself and plunging to its foundations. There was the gentle patter of falling debris, like light summer rain and a yawning creak as the house tried to hold onto the rest of its innards. But nothing else. Jack waited. And waited. Slowly he made his way downstairs, unaffected every time his ghostly foot came into contact with a piece of flooring that was no longer there. It did not affect his gait or slow his descent. On the ground floor he looked through the gaping wound, as he had done on his first night in the house. Amongst the plaster and old furniture were bright splashes of freshly spilled blood and viscera. Jack doubted there was any way either man could have survived being crushed by most of a house. In fact, he was betting on it.

Eventually a figure pulled itself out of the debris. It slid from between a hunk of plaster and the sharp, cracked-bone end of a support beam as though it had been poured through the gap. Its skin bore the same milky iridescence that his own form had taken on since he had become a spirit. Soon another form pooled from a gap at the edge of the room, seeping through the cracks. Slowly, laboriously both forms pulled themselves together, back into the shape of men. Jack waited until both ghosts were standing, looking around them at the carnage of the collapse before he cleared his throat and spoke, in the sweetest voice he could muster.

"Hello boys. Fancy seeing you here!"

THE BRACE POSITION

"Is there a doctor on board?" comes the slightly nasal announcement over the aeroplane's tannoy system.

Oh no. It's the announcement that I've dreaded any time we've ever flown anywhere. I *am* a doctor, but the thought of attending an unknown emergency thousands of feet in the air with the bare minimum of equipment fills me with dread. My surgery consists of coughs and colds, toddlers getting their immunisations, bunions and lanced boils. I have no interest in the fast-paced anxiety of emergency medicine and even less interest in having to improvise from a first aid kit and whatever medication the other passengers might have. I don't think my heart could take it anyway. Nerves bubble in my stomach, my pulse thuds in my ears, but my eyelids remain closed. If I'm lucky, there will be another doctor on board, someone younger, more gallant, less afraid, and I can carry on sleeping. That's selfish. I should probably go up, see if they need any help. Even if there is another doctor on board, two heads are probably better than one. An old saying, but true.

"If there is a doctor on board, please can they make themselves known to cabin crew." There is a note of hysteria behind the seemingly calm announcement from the flight attendant. It must be that no-one has volunteered their help. Guess that means I'm up. I try to open my eyes. They don't open. Everything is still black. I try to sit up in my seat, alert someone that I can't open my eyes. Maybe the ailment they're asking a doctor to attend to is catching. I can't move. I can't speak.

"I'm a doctor," I hear from beside my seat. It dawns on me suddenly and completely in the darkness that I am the emergency. The call out is for me. I can't open my eyes. Everything is black.

**

Light returns slowly. It bleeds into the edges of my vision, highlighting the capillaries in my eyelids, turning the world pink. Pink and clean like freshly scrubbed hands or like the holiday sunset that I have been looking forward to sharing with my wife. Finally, my eyes open. The door of the aircraft is agape, letting in the bright sunlight of the Caribbean. I can feel the heat of the sun, reflecting off the tarmac and seeping in through the open door as the paramedics wheel out my body on a stretcher. It's covered by one of the scratchy aeroplane blankets, but I recognise my shoes poking out of the bottom. My sobbing wife follows in its wake. I reach out to touch her, but my fingertips only graze the back of her shirt. Then the whole procession is gone. I'm still sitting in my seat – 23C.

Over the sound of aircraft engines from the open door, I can hear one of the flight attendants crying in the galley area. Her colleague is rubbing her back in soothing circles. The sound of his rough hand on the nylon of her uniform sets my teeth on edge. Maybe if I clear my throat they'll see me? No dice. I try shouting out, waving, even reaching my finger towards the 'summon attendant' button on the ceiling above me. It passes right through.

"You're wasting your time," a voice says behind me.

Swivelling round as fast as I can in the narrow seat, I look through the gap. Behind me is an old man, his face wizened and brown like a nut. He wears a gaudy Hawaiian shirt, jaunty bucket hat and a vintage camera slung around his sinewy neck. The entire ensemble looks terribly dated, something I might have seen in my parents' old holiday snaps.

"I've been tryin' to get someone's attention for years!" he says, laughing and shaking an empty plastic wine glass from side to side. "I'd do anything for a refill!" he cackles, displaying an open mouth missing more than a few teeth.

"Don't mind him, hun," comes a voice from a few rows ahead and to the right. "He thinks he's hilarious, but I've been hearing the same joke for years."

A lady stands up and gives me a solemn wave. I can still hear Nutty cackling away behind me. I'm nauseous. What is happening? I fumble with the seatbelt, unable to grasp the metal mechanism, my breath starting to hitch in panic.

"Ah, look what you've done now, Pete," says the woman from up front. "Why you gotta always make 'em panic?" she tuts loudly and Nutty-now-Pete's raucous giggles subside to a dusty sigh at the reprimand.

The woman makes her way back to me. Her legs are very swollen. She struggles to walk down the aisle towards me. Without a word she offers me her hand; her wrists are also swollen into painful looking bands and I can barely see her eyes in her puffy face. I'm still struggling with the belt.

She grabs my sweaty fingers and pulls. She is much stronger than she looks. I stand up, my body moving through the belt to stand upright in the tight row.

"There," she says assuredly. "See. There's no need for dramatics." It's the type of no-nonsense statement my grandmother used to make. A solid, sturdy woman who had no time for any kind of histrionics. "I'm Pam," she said, turning my hand in hers to force me into a handshake.

The pressure of her hand holding mine is calming. The social contract of never being rude in the face of someone else's hospitality helps to ground me in the moment.

"What? How? Whaa..," I manage through numb lips.

"You're dead!" Pam tells me matter-of-factly. "We're all dead," she says, gesturing around the plane. A few faces dotted around the rows look at me.

Pam explains the mechanics to me while the flight attendants ready the aircraft for its return journey. I'm never going to have my long-awaited Caribbean holiday. It's back to Heathrow for me. Pam sits next to me and tells me the story of every other member of The Dead Travellers. She makes them sound like a touring company or a monsters of rock band from the eighties. Pete died of old age and more than a little heart disease. Erica up in first class had an undiagnosed DVT that travelled up to her lungs but she doesn't like to socialise with those back in economy, Pam tells me, rolling her eyes.

"What about you?" I ask, feeling rather impolite. Pam doesn't seem to mind. She pats the back of my hand pleasantly and sighs.

"I'm the reason they don't give out complimentary bags of peanuts any more, hun," she says, a little wistfully. "Wasn't even my own fault. The closed air circuit," she says, swirling her hands in the air to demonstrate the route of the anaphylaxis-causing dust.

I feel a little sheepish. The lack of complimentary peanuts had been something I'd been bemoaning to my wife as they brought around the drinks trolley. I hope Pam hadn't heard me, but her comment doesn't seem pointed. Instead, she explains to me that for some reason our souls are bound to the plane even though our bodies have been taken away. We can make it to the doors, but no further, forever trapped in a metal tube between destinations.

I stand at the exit, the metal stairs so tantalisingly close but yet so far away. The heat of the Caribbean sun beams through me. I can almost feel its warmth. Looking down at my hand, I see the way the sun prisms through me, refracting slightly through my new ghostly visage. In the distance, on the outskirts of the airport, I can see gently waving palm trees against the painfully blue sky. It is like a beautiful painting kept behind a pane of glass. It isn't right! It isn't fair! I am so close! Maybe, I think a little unkindly, Pam just hasn't tried hard enough to get through.

Taking a couple of steps back, I focus on the open doorway. Sucking in two quick breaths to steady myself, I run full pelt at the square of blue in front of me. At the last possible moment, I push off with all my might from the utilitarian carpet, throwing myself into the balmy air, waiting to clear the doorway and revel in the fresh air beyond. It is like hitting a brick wall and a blender all at once. My atoms, my very essence is whisked apart, imploding like a dead star. There isn't enough left of me to scream, yet every cell seems to screech, stretched to their breaking points like a rubber band. The pain is a vice, gripping me tighter and tighter and as I think I can't take it anymore, that I might go mad from it, it begins to abate. Slowly I reconstitute, cell by atom by organ by limb, until I am sitting back in seat 23C, panting and wild. Pam looks at me sadly.

"Why didn't you tell me?!" I rasp at her in an accusatory manner.

"You wouldn't have believed me, hun. No-one believes it the first time. They have to experience it for themselves."

Shakily I stand, running my hands down my new ghostly body, hoping everything has come back as it should. The door still stands open. I could try it again, but the thought of it, the wrenching, searing pain of it is enough to stop me.

Soon the stairs begin to shake with returning passengers, sunburnt, tired and not looking forward to popping their perfect holiday bubble. They stow their hand luggage and take their seats. Even 23C has an occupant.

"All aboard!" shouts Nutty Pete, the outline of his ghostly body just visible around the new passenger sitting in his seat. "I hope they change the in-flight movie soon," he grumbles, "I've seen this one so many times I know all the words!"

This can't be it! I can't be destined to spend eternity sharing a too cramped economy seat with a stranger, learning all the words to the in-flight entertainment and safety demonstrations. I always wanted to travel the world but not like this! Pressed up against a tiny porthole to observe a sliver of blue and green past the tarmac or the flat black of night punctuated with the rhythmic heartbeat of orange lights of various airport support vehicles.

"Cabin crew prepare for take-off," comes over the tannoy system. I panic, standing in the aisle, desperate to be released, desperate to go back. Desperate. Pam pats the seat next to her, looking on sympathetically at my distress. When I don't come, she gets up, holds out her hands and takes my trembling ones gently in her warm, dry, swollen ones. She pulls me down next to her. The fight goes out of my body. I snuggle up to her and she wraps her warm arms around me, resting her cheek on the top of my head. I remember sitting next to my mother on the sofa as a child, desperate to avoid my bedtime and being left alone in the dark. She would hold me in the same way. I feel warm and safe. My eyes close. The pressure in the cabin changes. My ears don't pop, they don't exist anymore. Not really. And now neither do I. Not really.

A/S/L?

It is sometime in the middle of your school summer
holidays. You don't know when exactly. You are not even
sure of the date. Just that it is August. Looking at the
calendar would only draw your eye to the big red cross
when school starts again, and you don't want to think of
that. These are still the halcyon days of freedom before your
mum takes you to buy school supplies – the pencil case on
sale not the one you coveted every time you joined her at
the supermarket, an itchy woollen skirt from the school
supplies shop that you don't think you will ever grow into
and will spend a good five minutes rolling up every morning
and a branded jumper that you will instantly make thumb
holes in to pull the fabric over your hands.

You wake with the sun teasing the edges of the
curtains. The birds are already singing and the breeze
through your bedroom window smells of cut grass and the
warm tarmac of the road outside. Indeed, you can hear one
of the neighbours start their mower, to kick up even more
of the pungent summer scent into the air. There is no time
for a shower. Instead, you spray some *Charlie Red* liberally
around your neck line and onto the *Groovy Chick* shirt that
you got for your last birthday. Your parents aren't anywhere

to be found downstairs so you help yourself to the box of cereal on top of the cupboard and a glass of sweet, cold milk from the fridge. You eat faster than you would if there were an audience, wiping spilt milk from your chin with the back of your hand.

Last night, with the curly cord of the home phone looped around your arm like a hungry python, you agreed with your best friend Katie that you would go to hers the next day because her parents had just got the internet. You don't have it at home yet. Your only experience of it so far has been strictly chaperoned in school IT lessons. But Katie tells you her parents are both at work tomorrow and you can spend the whole day checking out the chat rooms and the websites your friends at school whisper about while you're in the cafeteria line. Attempting to access any of them in the computer lab results in a very large, very scary-looking notification to tell you that the site was definitely, unequivocally blocked. You always try to do it when the teacher is on the other side of the room, so they won't see the massive alert on your screen when you're meant to be utilising all the different types of *WordArt* for your presentation or making your way through the instructions to construct a graph in Excel.

Your bike is exactly where you left it, lying on its side on the parched grass of the back lawn. You can see drops of dew clinging to the reflectors on the spokes of the wheels. It's a bit too small for you now but you'll ride most of the way standing so your knees don't bash the bottom of the handle. There are already a lot of bruises on your knees, you've noticed as you scrutinise them in your nightly bath. They don't look like the knees of the popular girls in your class who have already started shaving the downy, golden hair that grows there and wouldn't be seen with a scab or a bruise above their knee-high socks. You will endeavour to make more of an effort when the new term starts but, for now, you're enjoying your summer too much.

Katie's bike is waiting on the front lawn as you pull up and you drop your own next to it. They'll be fine here till you and Katie pick them up again in a couple of hours, when you've become tired of staring at the screen and decide to go to the park to see if any boys from school are lounging around the playground. You don't mind some of them but most of them will be smoking and spitting because they don't like the taste or sharing around a large bottle of cheap cider that you think smells and tastes a lot like feet. You'd rather just ride your bike, gleeful as the wind lifted the sweaty hair off the back of your neck, watching your neighbourhood whizz past until it's time to go home for tea. You and Katie used to pelt down the hill at the far end of the park for hours on your bikes, pretending the juddering of the was the galloping of a mighty steed rather than a rickety Raleigh. You'd much rather still be doing that rather than flirting with grotty boys you see at school all week. But you'll do what Katie wants to do because she's your best friend and she gets a little moody when you tell her no and tells you that you need to grow up.

Katie's mum opens the front door to you. She only has one shoe on and is trying to put on the other while opening the door and cramming a piece of toast into her mouth at the same time. You thank her and slip past her fraught form into the living room where Katie is lying upside down on the sofa, her dark hair pooling on the carpet below her, as she watches cartoons. You sit next to her, neither of you saying much while you both listen to her mother crashing around as she gets ready for work. Finally, her mum flings open the living room door and tells you that she's leaving and to both be good. She doesn't wait for you to answer before she's at the front door, slamming it roughly. Katie stands up, her face red from being upside down for so long, and watches as her mother walks down the front path and gets in her car. You both listen to it roll down the driveway and take off into the distant place where adults go to work.

Satisfied that she is actually gone, you both go to the kitchen and fill up large glasses with fluorescent coloured pop that Katie's mum gets on special and always dyes your tongue a different colour, no matter which flavour you pick. Carefully, with both hands you take the glasses into the little alcove that Katie's father uses as a makeshift office and which holds the family computer. Katie presses the power button and the behemoth whirrs into life like a jet getting ready to take off. The Windows logo crashes onto the screen, the speakers of the computer set so high that the sound distorts as it bellows through the small alcove. Katie shrieks and spins the volume knob on each as quickly as she can. You both laugh nervously at each other, knowing that what you are doing is illicit, especially in the eyes of your parents.

Katie's parents had received a disc from AOL in the post that contained a few hours of free service. You hope your own parents will get a similar disc in the mail and be convinced that your household needs the internet too. Your dad only uses the computer to play Solitaire. Katie presses the button on the disc drive and a small hatch opens, the computer rolling out its plastic tongue to accept the offering of the disc. She obliges and you watch as she deftly double clicks the icon and inputs all the log in information. The computer begins the connection process, a series of chirps and chirrups and a long electronic warbling as the computer engages in the electronic handshake enabling it to connect to the internet.

Soon you have negotiated the site and logged into

one of the AOL chatrooms with the username BustyBetty69. It wasn't your choice but you got swept up in the moment and Katie was in fits of giggles so you agreed. You don't know why sixty-nine is funny and you don't want to ask because she'll only roll her eyes at you and you don't want to be uncool. There are a lot of people in the chatroom and almost immediately someone asks you 'A/S/L?'. You look to Katie for an explanation and as you expected she rolls her eyes at your lack of knowledge. She tells you it is to ask your age, sex and location. She decides that BustyBetty is a twenty-three year old flight attendant from London which sounds very glamourous to you, being a teenager from a small town, and obviously to a lot of men in the chatroom who message you to ask if you want to 'cyber'. You don't know what that means either but you've learnt your lesson in asking Katie to elaborate.

Katie tells the chatroom that you're new to the internet and what kind of things should you be checking out. There is a slew of pornographic recommendations, but within those is a website name that grabs your attention – DeathDiary. You tell Katie that you should check it out. The chatroom has not been as fun as you imagined. It doesn't seem that different from school, everyone trying to be mean for reasons you don't quite understand. Katie sighs dramatically but she exits the chatroom and opens up a new window.

The browser opens to a smiling cartoon butler asking you what you want to search for and with two fingers Katie types in 'Death Diary'. The cartoon butler obliges. The website is suitably macabre looking, all black backgrounds and dripping red text. It asks you to answer some basic questions and promises you that it will predict the date of your death based on these. Katie does not look convinced, but you pull the keyboard towards you and type in all the answers to its questions. You press enter. The loading wheel spins and spins. Finally, the screen changes and it tell you a date in the future that you will meet your demise. The date is so far in the future you wonder if you will have your own robot butler and take two weeks every year to go see your friends in the colony on Mars. It is not a scary number. You slide the keyboard back over to Katie.

Dubiously Katie enters her information and waits patiently for the same spinning bar that you did. The number arrives. It is not a date that brings up thoughts of robots or interstellar travel. It is not a date in the far future. The year is the same. The date is next month. All the saliva dries up in your mouth. You look over at Katie's stunned face. It is turning red. She turns to you and a hideous approximation of a laugh escapes her open mouth. It makes you feel strange. You no longer want to be in this stuffy alcove with the smell of hot dust coming from the back of the computer and the sickly-sweet pop curdling in your stomach. Katie tries the laugh again and tells you that it's just a stupid website, it doesn't mean anything. It's stupid and you're stupid for having suggested it. Mutely you nod in agreement with her. You look at the time in the bottom right of the screen and tell her that you need to go home. Katie does not say another word. Neither do you. You rush out of her house, grabbing your bike as you run and peddle as hard as you can, trying to outrun whatever it is you have witnessed in the once comforting sanctuary of Katie's suburban home.

*****

A notification pings. The loud trill of it sounds through the darkness in which the computer sits. A solitary sentinel. A skeletal hand appears from the inky blackness and clasps the hard plastic of the mouse. Clicks once. There is a new date and a new name on the screen. The hand's owner nods and makes a sound in the back of his throat, a noise of affirmation that sounds like a thousand souls simultaneously taking one last sucking breath before an eternity of screaming. Death doesn't feel anything for Katie. She is just another name to be added to his diary. The method of delivery may have changed but his job has not. Death has entered the digital age. It is not the only way that he collates his names, but Death is keeping up with the times. Death has modernised.

THE HAUNTED TABLE

As she sat at the solid wooden table, hunched over her laptop, the smell of burning crept from the kitchen to assault her nostrils. She couldn't remember putting anything on to cook, but it was entirely possible that she had and had forgotten about it. She'd been so distracted over the last few days from writing her proposal, that ordinary things kept turning up in the most incongruous of places – her keys in the fridge, her slippers left outside the back door to become soggy in the rain. Panicked, she uncurled herself from her seat, the lack of movement in the last several hours making her joints creak, and ran towards the kitchen. She slid round the corner in socked feet, ready to fish out a long forgotten piece of toast from the toaster or incinerated fish finger left under the grill.

As she entered the kitchen, she almost slid right into him – standing blackened and crisp in the middle of the tiled kitchen floor. Pieces of him drifted to its surface, like grey ash from a bonfire caught in a gentle breeze. His skin, what remained of it, was bubbled and scorched. It had split in places, showing something wet and oozing beneath. He listed wildly to one side, flesh contracted tight like a burnt pork chop to bring his shoulder close to his ear. She could see the charred bellows of his lungs working through the torn wall of his chest.

Maggie stepped back, opening her mouth to scream but the smell of him caught in the back of her throat, making her cough and rendering her mute as he stared at her with red and weeping eyes in exposed sockets. She could not take her own eyes off him as she struggled to regain her breath. A few wisps of dirty blond hair clung to his burnt scalp and a few scraps of fabric draped from his terrible limbs, but the rest of him was bare, naked. Not that it mattered. She had only thought of him as a man because of his height, his broad burnt shoulders and barrel chest. Scorching flame and unbearable heat had obliterated anything else that might have identified him as such. His nakedness was actually the least shocking thing about him. He opened his mouth, his tongue a black wiggling stump in his raw mouth, and moaned. The smell of burnt meat was stronger, seeming emanating from his very insides. It was a cooked stomach smell, like bad haggis left to fester on a counter in an abandoned house.

Swallowing hard, Maggie finally found her voice.

"TIM!" she yelled out, even though she had watched him leave for work hours ago.

She yelled because she didn't know what else to do and because she needed someone else to see what was in front of her. She needed proof that she hadn't gone suddenly, inexplicably mad.

The figure reared back at the sound of her cry, stumbling on unsteady legs, like scaffolding worn loose and rickety in a summer storm. He looked ready to drop small bones like hollow poles, letting the entire structure above tumble to the ground below. He hit the side of the butcher block counter, that she had been so pleased to have installed, and crumbled spectacularly to the floor like bacon bits with a puff of dirty, black smoke. She crept over to the place where he had stood, the burnt bits adhere hotly to the bottom of her cotton socks, indenting the soles of her feet like shards of hot coals. Crunching over the pile he had left, she cringed at the sound and sensation. It reminded her of accidentally stepping on snails and crushing their shells on the front path after a heavy downpour. It always made her desperately sad, wondering if that snail had a mate who was watching in horror, as well as terribly guilty for her crime. This crunch did not make her sad, it made her stomach revolt and hot saliva drench the back of her mouth. It was what she imagined the floor of the back room of the crematorium to be like, coated in small specks of detritus from the scores of people transferred from cremator to urn, all swept up together at the end of the day to be disposed of. Though surely the workers wouldn't be so careless as to drop little particles of people's loved ones in the middle of their day, would they? Either way, neither of those things were something she wanted to think about while walking across her brand new kitchen floor in the middle of the day.

Nothing else remained of her lunch time intruder apart from the scent of him clinging in a low cloud of smoke, tendrils of it already fingering the edges of the window, trying to find a way out. The low fug of it was cloying and she could taste it on the back of her tongue. The taste was oddly familiar. Charcoal. It brought to mind a summer BBQ, an inexperienced chef at the grill and biting into something burnt on the outside but strikingly, glaringly pink in the middle. Raw flesh caught between teeth. She hawked indelicately and spat into the deep marble sink that had cost them an arm and a leg to have installed. The flavour was still a ghost in her mouth, coating her tongue stickily. Flipping on the extractor fan to get rid of the remaining smoke, she crossed to the large American-style refrigerator and pulled a carton of juice out of its door. Pouring it into a glass would take too much time, and she was desperate, so she slugged from it directly, trying to banish the flavour from her mouth with sticky orange sweetness.

**

Tim had barely even put his backpack down when Maggie began to babble about the entity that had appeared in their kitchen that afternoon. Her words tumbled over themselves, getting caught in her mouth, making little sense. Irritation bubbled in him. He had wanted just a moment to get in the door, take off his shoes, maybe get a drink before having to deal with anything else. He had been dealing with people all day. Was it so much to ask for a little quiet? The evening commute also did not make him the most gregarious, and it was even longer now they had moved into this house. When they had begun house hunting, Tim had wanted something smaller, closer to town. Maggie had wanted a dilapidated farmhouse in the middle of nowhere. They had compromised on this place – a new build in a quiet seaside suburb but now full to the brim with Maggie's old-world style knick-knacks and shabby chic furniture.

Tim hadn't realised how expensive old things could be. Weren't they just things that people wanted to get rid of? Or things that had been donated en masse to charity shops upon the death of their owners? Tim liked things to be new and shiny but marriage is a myriad of compromises and so he'd chosen the chrome American-style refrigerator in the kitchen and she the wooden butcher block counters. He had managed to wrangle her into accepting a ridiculously large television in the living room and she, in turn, had insisted on the behemoth of a dining room table at which she was currently sitting, babbling at him about a crispy ghost in their new kitchen. The table had come from a local furniture maker who had constructed the enormous piece from reclaimed wood courtesy of the local pier that had burned down a few months prior. The thought of owning a piece of history had enchanted Maggie. Tim would have been happy enough to buy something new and flat packed from Ikea. But since it was going to be Maggie's desk as well as their dining table, she had the final say.

Once she had slowed down enough for Tim to understand her properly, he scoffed at her assertions that their brand new house was haunted. It was a new build, no one had lived in it before them. It was virginal. No-one had had the chance to die in it yet, unless the developers were being very cagey about their health and safety record. Hauntings were for old stately manors or country cemeteries holding the bones of sickly Victorians, not for choose your own floor plans and home builder warranties. He listened as she rattled on and on even as he stood, determined to get a stiff drink from the kitchen. He gripped Maggie's shoulder as he walked past, as close as he would usually come to showing any outward affection to her or anyone else. Public displays of affection were simply not in his nature.

Maggie wanted to lean her head into him as he stood behind her, experience the comforting warm weight of him for as long as possible. But as soon as the contact came, it was gone again. She often wondered why she had married someone who was so stingy with affection. He had never been one for cuddling or hand holding, always seeming tense and more than a little embarrassed when she reached for his hand in public. It always left her feeling a little chagrined, like a child who had been told off for being too exuberant. The same had been true about cuddling after sex. She wanted them just to be together for a moment, bathing in the afterglow of their lovemaking, but she could feel how antsy he was under her touch, heart beating hard under her hand, shuffling and twitching before she released him. His relief was almost palpable as he rose from the rapidly cooling bed to jump in the shower and wash the smell of her off him. It often left her a little sad. And a little used. In the early days of their relationship, she had tried to cuddle up to him at night, thinking he might be a bit more amenable in his sleep. But he had kept her awake all night, twitching and jumping like a puppy having a nightmare and shocking her back to wakefulness every time she began to drop off. She gave up and slept on her own side, no longer crossing the invisible divide down the centre of the bed. Even so, Maggie would give anything to be held right now, enveloped in a warm hug and told everything would be OK rather than feeling a little stupid and more than a little scared.

He walked into the kitchen, took a beer from the fridge and began removed ingredients for dinner, putting each one down a little harder than was necessary to communicate his disappointment that she had not started preparing his meal before his return from work. There was no cry of shock or horror at a visceral apparition, just the slam of ingredients, the clang of pans being taken out of the cupboard and the rhythmic click of the gas stove being turned on. Maggie didn't want food. The thought of it made her nauseous. Despite drinking the whole carton of juice, her mouth still tasted like the crispy intruder whose pieces she had hastily swept into a dustpan and dumped into the outside bin before Tim had got home. Tiny particles of him would now be clinging to the sticky residue of yoghurt pots or mingling with the grounds from the coffee machine. She wouldn't be able to prove their existence to Tim without sifting through the trash for each tiny individual crispy shard, and dumpster diving was not going to make her look more credible. She watched Tim for a while, his broad back moving between chopping board and pan, dumping in the ingredients to sizzle in the hot oil. There was a sharp scent of onions in the air. Tim removed a packet of chicken breasts from the fridge and she desperately fought the urge to retch. The flesh was slick, pearly pink, and glistening. Maggie caught a whiff of the intestinal burp of the air from the packet as Tim savaged the plastic film with an inappropriately large knife. It smelled sickeningly similar to the ghost's earlier cry. She could not face the idea of meat. The thought of cooked flesh made her stomach turn.

"I'm going to take a bath," she announced, not giving Tim a chance to reply to ask her a million questions about whatever dish he was going to half-arse for their dinner tonight. She didn't care, she wasn't going to eat it anyway.

Closing the door of the bathroom with a satisfying click, she began to run the bath. Maggie selected the most floral smelling bubble baths and bath salts from the collection on top of the medicine cabinet. The scents of lavender and white musk and ylang-ylang filled the bathroom as they infused the water, creating crests of thick white bubbles on the surface. Leaving the tub to fill, she went through the adjoining door into their bedroom and stripped off, leaving her clothes in a pile at the foot of the bed. She knew it annoyed Tim, but tonight she frankly didn't care.

The bathroom was full of steam when she re-entered, but instead of relaxing floral notes, the fog was full of the brackish smell of salty, stagnant water. The tub was no longer clean and bubbly but dank and silty, green like an old bog or forgotten pond deep in the woods. The fermented scent wound its way into her hair and tickled the small hairs in her nose. Leaning precariously over the porcelain rim, she peered into the murky depths of her freshly run bath. Instead of her own face looking back at her, she saw the crispy visage of her afternoon intruder. His eyes were wide open, the whites as grey as overcooked boiled eggs. At the bottom of the bath, just visible through the murky water, was a brownish-red skeleton.

"THE TABLE!" came the words, bubbling up through the water and bursting on its surface with a meaty burp.

At the first screams, Tim left the chicken stir-fry to burn on the stove and raced up the stairs. The pungent scent of expensive cosmetics and the shrieking wail of his naked wife assaulted him as he flung open the bathroom door, which smacked against the wall, removing a small chunk of new build plaster. He couldn't however see any bones in the bath and he could make no sense of her cries about a table. Maybe Maggie had lost her marbles? He was half tempted to call a doctor or an ambulance, anything to stop her screams as she pressed herself against his shirt in the damp bathroom, her sobs wracking through his chest. Eventually he was able to manoeuvre her to the bedroom, pulling on her pyjamas as though dressing an overwrought child and installing her under the heavy duvet to sob alone in the dark.

**

He did not expect to return from work the next day

to find the house empty of Maggie and a suspicious absence where the dining room table had stood. On the floor in its place was page after page of print-outs from the internet on the fire that had burned down the pier several months beforehand. It had happened well before they had moved to the area, but Tim remembered the story as part of the furniture maker's spiel when they had bought the table. The articles revealed that a group of youths had intentionally set the fire late one night, resulting in the tragic death of a man who was drunkenly sleeping on the pier. A solid wall of flame had blocked his exit in all directions. He could not even throw himself from the side into the water below. Tim shuddered at the thought of burning alive. They had retrieved the man's bones and whatever else remained of his body from the water below, along with the detritus from the pier. Why would anyone make a souvenir from the wood from a crime scene? Tim thought, aghast. If they'd known, they would never have bought it. Maybe Maggie was right, and the wood had absorbed the essence of a murdered man.

Scouring the house for Maggie, he became aware of the smell of smoke and a crackling sound from their back garden. Stepping over the drag marks in the carpet, he opened the patio doors and walked out into the cold night air. Maggie stood in front of a raging bonfire, watching the embers from their ridiculously expensive, but ridiculously cursed, dining table float into the frosty night sky. The smell of lighter fluid was heavy and acrid in the air, turning the smoke black and pungent. She turned to face him, the orange light crackling in her too-bright eyes. Ash clung to her thin pyjamas, dotted across her chest like a constellation, and her bare feet were turning blue on the patio stones despite the heat of the blaze. Undeterred, Maggie was smiling and clasping her hands together, as happy as a child on bonfire night. Tim instinctively raised his head, looking for fireworks, but the only screams to be heard were emanating from his wife's mouth.

"HE'S FREE!" Maggie yelled into the night sky. "FREE. FREE. FREEEEE!"

54

CIRCLE OF PESTILENCE

My name is Mallory, and I am thirty-six years old. I will always be thirty-six years old. I died on a wet, drizzly morning at the end of August to the sound of the hitching beep of a heart monitor and the crying of my husband. The last thing I ever saw was a droplet of rain slipping down the pane of the hospice's window, as unstoppable as the tears slipping down Paul's face. The garden beyond the window was lush and full, lapping up the rain in the hazy light of late summer.

It sounds like the end of an inspirational made-for-TV movie, doesn't it? All sweeping strings and hazy camera filters to show the brave woman, so serene, so heartening, coming to terms with the end of her life and slipping away into the great goodnight with loving words for her husband. That wasn't me. From the moment of my diagnosis, I was furious. I didn't take up yoga or meditation; I was too mad. I didn't have a bucket list because I was too sick. I didn't try to be mindful or come to terms with it. I just got angry. So angry I hoped I would burn out my sickness with rage, but I think I just provoked it further.

I didn't swallow my pride and tell my husband that it was okay to move on and find love again. I told him that if he slept with anyone else, I would haunt the shit out of him and kick him in the balls every time he lowered his pants. He had started to laugh until he saw my face. My face that was deadly, completely serious. I wanted him to mourn me forever. To keep a picture of me next to the bed to scare off other women. If I wasn't going to get my happily ever after, then he sure as hell wasn't going to have one either. Dying didn't make me a nicer person; it made me into a bit of a bitch, if I'm being honest. I think Paul was secretly relieved when the doctor suggested I check into a hospice so he didn't have to deal with both his guilt and my unmitigated fury.

After I died and woke up in the other place, my anger came with me. I wasn't grateful to be out of pain; I was apoplectic that I had died so young. I shouted and screamed and cried as much as you can do without a body. It scared the daylights out of the welcoming committee, and they slunk away with their overly rehearsed speeches and fluffy little hugs. I snarled and hissed and curled myself into a little vibrating ball of energy, sparks and all. I did not conduct myself well when I first arrived, and I'm not even sorry about it.

Since I've been here, I have spoken to so many people who come across all zen and enlightened, but after spending any kind of meaningful time with them, they invariably start telling me about their regrets or missed opportunities. They are just as regretful and bitter as I, and even that did not give me any solace. Someone else's dreamy-eyed recollections of all the missed moments really starts to pale when you have a plethora of your own. There are only so many platitudes before the whole conversation becomes bromidic.

I tried to keep to myself but that became too boring; there is nothing here but oodles of time and lots of mopey old gits telling you about the girl that got away. Whenever I could, I liked to go hang out with Death. As you can imagine, he's pretty busy, but he stops by now and again, and he's the only person here that I can stand. Death is always followed by a miasma of feral cats. They're not like pet cats; they don't have a human soul to attach themselves to once they die, so they tend to follow Death. He'd hate to admit it because he loves his cold and uncaring image but Death has a special place in his not-heart for feral cats. He's always loved cats ever since he was weighing feathers and hearts in ancient Egypt. He loves their aloofness, their unwavering loyalty to themselves, and their opportunistic nature.

When Death is around, he makes great company. He doesn't want to tell you all of his regrets. He doesn't even want to tell you about his day. When Death is back in the office, he likes to play chess. I never played chess in life and I'm pretty awful at it in death. It doesn't help that Death is a grandmaster; he's very good at seeing the consequence of actions. For me, it wasn't even really about the game. When Death and I played chess, it was quiet. He'd stare at the board, his hand dipping into the swirling cloud of purring, hissing, meowing cats at his ankles, his bony hand stroking whoever placed themselves below it. The stroking motion of his hand was a soothing metronome in a place where no one can shut up for five minutes.

Our chess dates stopped when one of the souls that potters around here let slip that we can watch the living and see what they are doing. I had been an avid TV watcher in life, and as I watched Paul at my funeral, I knew I was hooked. At the wake, I was pleased to see him batting away the opportunistic hand of our neighbour as it crept up his thigh in a thinly veiled attempt to comfort him. Paul and I had always joked and called her 'Raunchy Rachel' because of the positively obscene outfits she wore to peg out the washing. I had laughed along at the time but had kept an eye on that sneaky cow—all milky thighs and big doe eyes whenever she came over to ask Paul to fix a leaky tap or some other such nonsense. I was glad when she stalked past the brown buffet of sausage rolls and cocktail sausages, back to her house. If I could, I would have spat.

I missed Paul. A lot. I would sneak off to watch him all the time. He was like my new favourite soap opera. I knew Paul was going back to work and I wanted to eavesdrop on all the lovely things he might say about me to his colleagues. He was still in the first stages of grief, almost like a honeymoon, where the memory of me was rose-tinted and almost exalted. He'd forgotten what a messy person I was, how annoyed he'd get when I would leave old receipts dotted around the house like confetti, or how I always rolled my leggings when I took them off and he had to fight with them before getting them in the washing machine. He'd forgotten what a pain in the arse I had been at times, and my loss was still too recent for anyone to say anything other than splendid things about me to him. It was a plethora of compliments, and I enjoyed it much more than was probably healthy or considered humble.

Hearing Paul talk about me and seeing how cut up he was about my death was pleasing at first but time really does seem to heal all wounds. For Paul at least; I still felt as raw as an open wound. Paul was starting to get over me. I could see it in the way he wasn't reduced to tears by finding an old bit of paper I'd stuffed into the back of the sofa because I couldn't be bothered to go to the bin while watching TV. He had laughed indulgently, scrunched it into a ball and thrown it away. It made me feel uneasy. I was too used to the effect of my loss being devastating to him and finding comfort in that. I had nothing to move on to; I was at the final stretch and I was bored and lonely and miserable. I felt like we were in our own little bubble, wrapped in a grief blanket while he was alone in the house. It reminded me of lazy Sunday mornings when we lounged around in bed together, listening to the birds out of the window and catching up on current events on our phones before finally dragging ourselves out of bed. He was no longer enjoying the quietness of our home where he could take my clothes out of the wardrobe and breathe in my smell. He had bagged everything up and taken it to the charity shop. Now, he was going out for Friday night drinks after work. He'd come home drunk and weaving and sometimes fall asleep on my side of the bed. Sometimes, he'd come home and stick the stereo on full blast— something I'm sure Raunchy Rachel was happy about at just gone midnight. I heard him on the phone to his mother, talking about whether he should get a dog for a bit of company. I didn't like this show anymore; it wasn't full of people being nice about me all the time and Paul would move on, I knew it deep down in my not-gut.

Paul did get a dog. He'd wanted one ever since I'd known him but we'd never gotten one. Another one of my life regrets; not making Paul happy with a dog. He was a scraggly looking thing from a shelter, but as soon as Paul got him home, he crawled into his lap and licked his cheek with a face full of doggy gratitude. Paul was smitten. The show had changed from 'how great my poor dead wife was' to 'man's heart mended by faithful mutt'. I was jealous all over again, watching their autumn walks through crunchy leaves followed by a pint in our once-favourite village pub. He even took the dog on bloody holiday; a walking holiday in the Lake District, where Paul did a lot of staring off into the distance with a silly little smile on his face.

I knew, of course, that it was going to happen but it didn't make it any less painful when Paul finally met someone. His dog had eaten a chicken bone and he had rushed it to the emergency vet's. The emergency vet was blonde and kind with a love for all animals in her heart. What a cliché. She had rubbed his back with little soothing circles when he had broken down in tears of happiness after hearing the dog was going to make it. He had looked up at her with watery admiration, a lot like the dog had done when he had first brought him home, and I knew once again that Paul was smitten. Shit. He had brought her flowers to thank her for saving his faithful friend, and the rest was kismet. They dated, and I seethed. I should have found something else to do; I should have gone and watched anyone else in the world—what the Dalai Lama really says when he stubs his toe, what Trump's hair looks like when he first gets up in the morning, Brad Pitt in the shower—but I stayed and watched the love of my life fall in love with a woman named Fey.

I thought I had been angry when I died. Now, I was inflamed. I rage-watched their daily adventures. I would have ground my teeth down had I any. I tortured myself with watching their new Sunday morning rituals, and I battered myself bloody by watching them make love, recognising Paul's moves that he had used with me and noting with alarm the new ones he was using with Fey. I even watched them as they slept, her head on the arm he curled protectively around her. My man was moving on and I wasn't. I was stuck and it was their fault.

My birthday rolled around and Fey decided to take Paul away on a little break for it. She told him it was to take his mind off of it, but I knew it was to assert her dominance. She worked with animals all day; she knew all about pissing out territories. She'd booked a little wood cabin, and as Paul, Fey and the dog walked into the cosy living room, I knew instantly she had done her homework— this place was perfect for Paul. It was quaint, homely and warm. She wasn't so crass that she would pop open the champagne but as they snuggled on the sofa in front of a crackling fire with the dog gently snoring at her feet, I knew this would be what Paul would think of on the date of my birthday going forward, not me, not our life together or the one we never got to finish together. I wished I still had eyes to cry because I felt so full of abject loneliness and hurt, I thought I might burst like a little black rain cloud. I stood at the edge of the ether and screamed; I screamed as hard as my non-lungs would allow me to. The fire flickered and Fey's fringe lifted away from her perfect, pixie face.

I stopped screaming. Had I done that? Had the force of my pain and sadness and rage commuted itself to an actual physical presence? No one had told me I could do that! What a bloody swindle! I thought watching the living was purely a one-way experience, like watching an incredibly painful movie about a life you'd never have. I didn't know I could have any influence over it. Fey went to check if there was a window open anywhere, and I laughed and laughed and laughed at her expression when she could not find one. This was the first time I had felt anything near happiness in the time since my death, and now I was truly obsessed.

The amount I had followed Paul before looked like a casual hobby compared to how I started to watch him and Fey after the cabin incident. There were no conversations with other spirits, no chess with Death; I'd even forgotten how annoyed I was with the big man in the office for my premature departure from Earth. I practised my newly acquired skill all the time. I started with a gentle breeze that would waft through the house, sometimes strong enough to wake the dog from its snoring slumber in his basket. Revivified, I ramped up my efforts until I could move small objects across a surface. I was jumping for joy—well, as much as someone who doesn't have a body can jump—when I managed to slide Paul's cufflinks along the surface of the dresser and into the bin on the floor. They were a present I had gotten him for a long-ago birthday. I felt fizzy with excitement as I watched his frustration mount as he fruitlessly searched for them. I took to being a petty problem in their house like a duck to water, hiding the top of the milk when one of them wanted a coffee, moving the dog's lead when he was already barking with excitement at going for a walk, and the old classic of moving the car keys. Finally, I was enjoying myself and all it took was being a royal pain in the arse. Be still my curdled heart!

I felt so much better having a project; learning something new can really give you a renewed purpose. The added bonus of my poltergeist activity was that it was really affecting Paul and Fey's relationship. They were snippy with each other, each blaming the other for moving the objects that I had skittered across the kitchen or bathroom counter earlier in the day. They were tired from being continually woken by a breeze that numerous tradespeople could not fathom the source of.

Both were leaving for work in the morning with bags under their eyes. Fey left one morning with odd shoes because she was too late to find the other one which I had tossed under the stairs. I was having the time of my afterlife. I was sure this was going to be enough to get them to finally break up and for Paul to go back to mooning over my loss. I rubbed my imaginary hands together like a movie mob boss. We could go back to our solitary cocoon, just me and him and maybe the dog. I was magnanimous enough to let him keep the dog at least. I never tried to wind up the dog if I could help it—that felt especially cruel, even for my now little black heart.

I was absolutely convinced that Paul was going to break up with Fey as I settled in to watch them driving down the motorway after visiting his mother. The visit itself had been excruciating; I had cringed with second-hand embarrassment just watching them. Paul's mother obviously thought it was time for him to move on. I knocked all her shampoo bottles into the bath for that slight, as she was making terribly obvious hints about impending nuptials and wedding bells in the future. Every torturously heavy hint had sent Paul's eyes jittering away from Fey's face and more than a few times sent him skittering away into the kitchen to make yet more cups of tea. They must have both been positively sloshing by the time they left her house to make the long drive home.

The atmosphere had been so agonising at Paul's mother's house that I was sure Paul was about to tell Fey he had made a mistake, that it wasn't working out, that he wasn't ready and that maybe they should call it a day. Fey herself was visibly annoyed and/or desperate for a wee. I'd been watching them for a while, and now felt like a verifiable Fey expert but even I couldn't differentiate the two needs on her face.

"What?" she spat at him after he had cleared his throat for a second time. "What is it Paul? Spit it out. If you want to break up with me, you're actually going to have to man up and say the words" Fey said, arms crossed, her whole body turned to look at the scenery speeding by.

Paul started laughing, proper relief laughter from his belly; the kind of guffaws you manage when you step back onto the pavement in time to dodge a speeding car. I'm sure if I'd still had a face it would have looked as confused as Fey's did as she whipped round to face him.

"Are you kidding me right now? What the fuck Paul?" she shouted as he banged his hand over and over again on the steering wheel. Tears of laughter slipped down the side of his face.

"You stupid goose," he managed. I bristled; it had once been his nickname for me. Talk about recycling. I didn't even warrant a lifetime nickname. Couldn't she get her own bird-related nickname? *Bin chicken* or *blue-footed booby*, I thought meanly.

"I don't want to break up with you. I want to marry you!" he shouted in the confines of the car, his voice bouncing around the space, deafeningly.

"Well, I want to marry you too!" Fey yelled back at him, matching tears streaming down her face. They both started laughing and whooping. Their words sliced me in two.

It was too much. It was overwhelming. Their shouting, their joy, their pure aliveness was too much for my sour little heart. I shrieked and screamed and rolled and roiled in the confines of my spiritness. I poured all my jealousy, rage and self-loathing into a scream that was so deep it seemed to rumble, like peals of thunder. For a moment, for one wonderful moment, the force of my ire put me with them in the car. I could feel the fabric beneath me, could smell Paul's horrible cologne—something I had joked he probably bought by the case because the shop couldn't get rid of it. I could have caressed his cheek. I could have tried to hold him close. I could have shown him all the love I struggled to in my last weeks. I could feel the tickle of his hair against my lips as I brought them to his ear. I could have told him how much he meant to me but instead I screamed every profanity I could think of as loudly as I could in the all too familiar shell of his ear.

Paul squawked and jerked away from the noise,

pulling the steering wheel with him. He was tired, frazzled from the weeks of my haunting, and he couldn't remember you had to steer into a skid, not away from it. He yanked the wheel left and right, panicking as the wheels locked and the car slid into the lane next to them. I felt the impact of cars either side of them. Sickening crunches made me wince as the metal chassis became dented from their speed, turning Paul's car into a deadly pinball. I felt the moment of weightlessness as the momentum of the car caused it to tip, rolling it down the motorway. The car was a missile of curling metal, shattering glass, screams, and the smell of hot blood and flesh. I saw the central reservation rush towards the windscreen, and the car came to a nauseating, crumpled stop, its careening roll broken by the thick metal of the reservation barriers. All I could hear was the gentle pitter patter of blood falling from their prone bodies onto the bed of glass covering the inside of the roof. No more screaming, no more breathing.

The other place was very quiet when I returned to my not-body on that side. Death was not at his table. The miasma of cats curled and mewled to one another, awaiting his return. I was pretty sure I knew the job he was on his way to. I had no one to speak to, to tell them the jumble of words that were spilling through my thoughts. I had spent so long watching The Paul and Fey Show that I didn't have any friends here. I was lonelier than I had been on Earth. For the second time, I hadn't come to terms. I waited. I waited until I heard someone calling my name.

To say Paul and Fey were not happy to see me would be an understatement. They now know I am the reason they are no longer planning their wedding, making a family or walking their dog in dappled woodland hand in hand. They watch the dog often. Neither of their families could bear to keep him, so he's with a nice new family now, bouncing around their brood of kids, knocking their smiling, smeared faces with his fiercely wagging tail. It doesn't bring them any comfort, like watching them did not bring any to me, but there is no way I will tell them that. I don't think any advice I have about the other place is worth a jot to them. I can feel their hatred towards me; it's visceral even in this place that should be fluffy clouds and love 24/7. I hated them for living, and now they hate me for dying. We've got a long time together, locked together in this circle of pestilence. It's going to be a very long eternity. Very, very long.

Originally published in 'Beyond The Grave: A Short Story Anthology' by Monnath Books – 31st October 2021.

THE FABLE OF CAREFUL WISHING

In the Pinkleton family manor house, in the middle of the English countryside, there lived a ghost. Alexander was a friendly little ghost who spent his time wafting between the rooms; out through the parlour and into the sitting room. Up the stairs and into the master bedroom. Down the hall. Into the guest bedroom. Through the en-suite and back into the corridor again. He floated up and down the stairs and sometimes warmed himself by sitting in the window reading nook to let sunbeams illuminate the dust motes floating through his body. Most of the time, he was a happy little ghost. There were no more lessons to do, or chores to complete, or nannies to scold him. But, more and more, Alexander was a very lonely little ghost. There was simply no-one to talk to.

Little Lord Pinkleton used to be able to see him, often pointing to Alexander with a chubby finger. But then Little Lord Pinkleton had remarked on seeing Alexander in his father's study and his nanny had spanked him silly for making excuses for being where he shouldn't. After that, Little Lord Pinkleton had pretended not to see Alexander and, after he'd gone away to Eton and returned to take up the mantle of Lord of the Manor, he hadn't been able to see Alexander at all. Now he and Lady Pinkleton were gone. Alexander had heard them talking about tax evasion and creative accounting, but he didn't understand a word of it. They had packed up all their belongings and left the manor. Alexander was all on his own.

The Pinkletons had left great white sails over all of their furniture to keep the dust motes from landing on it. Little Alexander was often afraid as he floated from the kitchen into the main parlour. They had draped all the familiar shapes, making them faceless and unfriendly. There were no noises in the house, not a boiling kettle or the soothing rumble of a TV turned up too loud. Alexander was lonelier than ever. He wished and wished there was someone to talk to. Alexander was very sad.

He didn't feel any better when the house was full of contractors banging and crashing through the rooms. Grown-ups could never see him and these grown-ups were far too busy to see a small ghost in a window reading nook, no matter how bright the sun was or how much dust their work kicked up into the air to float through his little ghostly body. But soon, once they had turned all the rooms into bedrooms with en-suite bathrooms and filled the parlour with circular tables with crisp, white tablecloths, they opened the doors of the manor again and the house filled with noise.

Alexander almost didn't go to see what all the fuss was about. He wanted to sulk and pout and hide in his favourite spot, curled under the third-floor radiator like a spoiled house cat, but before he could float up there, he heard them. Children. Lots and lots of other children, all making their way into the house. He did not know what a B&B was, or a half-term, having never been to school, but he was glad that whatever it was it had brought lots of children for him to play with. Alexander spent the next few months having a lovely time with all the living children. Sometimes he would come up behind them as they ate breakfast with their parents in what had once been the main parlour and blow just behind their ears. They would swat at him and he'd dance between the tables, laughing and clapping his hands with glee. Sometimes he would wake them up when they were sleeping to play tug with the bedclothes or jump up and down on the sides of their beds to rouse them. Sometimes, if he was feeling very, very naughty, and no-one was paying him enough attention, he would muster up all the strength he had and pinch one of the children swiftly on their arm or leg. Nanny would have told him off, but Alexander thought it was very, very funny. He'd done the same thing when he had been a living boy to his brothers and sisters. He'd always found it very funny. Even if they cried.

Soon, the number of visitors started to slow down. Lots of adults came into the house with fancy gadgets, stood in his favourite spots and talked about spikes on their EMF meters or walking through cold spots. Two grown-ups came and told them that they weren't getting any bookings because no-one wanted to stay in a haunted B&B. Alexander was sad that there were no more children to play with. He sulked and pouted and cried fat, sullen tears, but that didn't make him feel any better. He shrieked and hissed and kicked at the furniture, making all the adults gasp. That made him feel much better. Finally, they went away and Alexander could float back through the house as much as he pleased. But he was still terribly lonely. He wished someone would come back.

No-one came back to the house for weeks. Until one day, a man in a long black tunic, wearing a big cross around his neck, came to the house. Alexander was pleased. He'd had no-one to play with for so long. He didn't even mind that it was a grown-up. His excitement was so great that his footsteps made a sound on the stairs as he hurtled down them to play with the man. The man must have heard because he turned and when Alexander got to the bottom of the stairs, the man flicked liquid from a little vial in Alexander's direction. Some of it landed on his hand. It hurt. Alexander stamped and shouted, making the floorboards creak. So the man threw more liquid at him, intoning quickly from a small black leather-bound book that he was holding.

The liquid and the words made Alexander feel funny. He didn't want to play with this man after all. Alexander wanted to go back to his hiding place and wait for more children to come back to play. But as he went to float up the stairs, his legs didn't want to work. He could not move forward. He could not move backwards, either. As the man talked and talked, Alexander found that he couldn't move at all. Looking down, Alexander realised that he was beginning to dissolve. It started at his feet, then his legs, and soon the man's words were puncturing holes all over his little ghost body. Before he was fully gone, Alexander looked around the house that had been his home for decades. If only. If only he had been careful about what he wished for.

IRENE

Irene wasn't particularly religious, but ever since she had been a young girl she had heard the voices of the dead. They clamoured at the edges of her peripheral vision, pulled on her hands, sobbed and begged for her help. Their thoughts would come to her unbidden during a moment of reflection, a brief lull in normal conversation and in the nether-world between awake and dream. The spirits perched on the edge of her bed, the edge of the bath, the edge of her seat, the edge of her consciousness, and told her about their regrets, the things they hadn't done, the things they wished they could say. She felt their memories as if they were her own—a last embrace at the hospice, a late-night phone call about a tragic accident, the tone of a flat line on a hospital monitor, the feel of a cold gun at her temple. She wept in the depths and chasms of other people's memories, gathering them up like fishing nets, pulling them back, feeling the remembrances like barbs tearing through synapse, nerve, and muscle. She absorbed their stories and relived their sorrows in her dreams, until she woke keening.

Irene began to feel like a ghost herself, with no

space for a life of her own, crowded out by the lives of the dead. She was constantly hounded by their presence, constantly choking back tears that she didn't know belonged to her or a stranger. She didn't know what to do.

And then she did.

She sat at the bus stop one morning and thought about how she would do it, how she would join their ranks. She wasn't too far from the coast; she could drown herself. But she abhorred the thought of not knowing where she would end up, washed up one morning fish-nibbled and naked for a morning jogger to stumble over. She needed something a bit more intimate and much more clothed. At home, so only a policeman would find her when the smell started to bother the neighbours. Yes, that would do nicely.

She was so caught up in her plans, she hadn't noticed the spectre sit between herself and another young woman waiting with her on the bench.

"She was going to be my wife," the spectre mused. "That girl there. She didn't know yet, mind, but I had it all planned out. I had the ring bought and everything."

Irene sighed; closing her eyes did not block out the sound of his narrative

"I'd put it in the inside pocket of my best suit, all pressed and hanging in my wardrobe for that night, so I wouldn't lose it. I booked a table at a nice restaurant and I went to work. I was in such a rush on my way home on the bike to get dressed, I didn't see him turning."

"Stop it" Irene whispered. The lady next to her flicked her a look.

"Didn't seem him turning and then BANG!" He clapped his hands together and Irene jumped. "Right into his bonnet. All over his bonnet, in fact, but all I could think of was that ring sitting in my jacket pocket at home."

Irene began to cry.

"Did you hear me? It's in my bloody jacket pocket, just sitting there in the wardrobe and she hasn't bloody found it! Look at me! Look at what became of my plans, my dreams!"

The young man turned his head towards Irene, revealing his caved in skull, his eye viscous and bulging.

"Stop it! Stop it! Why can't you leave me alone? Why is this my problem?" She stood up and turned to the startled woman next to her. "He wants you to know that it's in his jacket pocket, the inside one, in his best suit hanging in the wardrobe. Oh, and he was a bloody idiot for driving so fast."

She barely managed to register the look of agonized shock on the woman's face before she began to run. She just wanted to outrun their pain and be alone with her own.

Irene made it back to her flat, sweaty and resolved. She had no one in her life that she needed to make peace with; no friends, no close co-workers. Her ever-oblivious parents were sunning themselves as ex-pats in the Costa-del-Wherever, phoning only once every couple of months. She wouldn't leave a note; she would just do it, tonight She would finally find some silence. The thought of infinite silence made her smile, released a weight inside her chest.

She marched into her bathroom and opened the medicine cabinet. She carried the bottles through to the bedroom in her arms and dumped everything out on the duvet, scattering them like confetti. She didn't have a lot, some Tramadol left over from a tweaked back, Ibuprofen, Paracetamol, Feminax, Vitamin C, but she planned to use it all. She wanted to be sure..

Irene looked at the pills, spread like fallen petals on the bed, and decided they might not be enough without alcohol. She proceeded to get sloppily, mournfully drunk, not bothering to put on the light as the evening sank into night. Around midnight, she felt the mattress give as someone perched beside her. She turned to the familiar biker, who was looking at her with the good side of his face.

"Oh Christ, really?" she shouted. "Couldn't you even have the decency to let me kill myself alone? You're all bloody voyeurs!" Next doors' neighbours banged on the wall.

The young man placed his hand over hers, the sensation was cold, an icy mist.

"She found it you know. Because of you, she decided to have a look, she went back to our house and she found the ring. I watched her pull it out and put it on. She was crying, but in the end she smiled, after cursing me a bit, well, a lot, actually" The ghost coughed out a laugh. "I hope she knows how much I really loved her, even if sometimes I was a bloody idiot like you said. That was thanks to you that was. If you didn't go all raving loony out there, that suit and that ring might have ended up in the charity shop and she might only have thought of me as that idiot who left her with no goodbye and a crumpled motorbike."

Irene looked up at his road-ravaged face.

"I'm trying to say thank you."

She glared at him through involuntary tears. He gestured to the pills strewn over the bed.

"They won't leave you alone if you're dead, you know. You'll have to hear their stories all the time. Imagine being in a doctor's waiting room for eternity with the whiniest old codgers you could find with no sense of personal space." Irene snorted a little laugh through her tears. "That's what it's like, a bad case of terminal regret."

He patted her hand once more and was gone.

Irene awoke the next morning, shaky and sick from her hangover. The dead were always full of regret, but she had actually helped one of them. She wanted to try to help some of the others, not just be passively bombarded by their burdens. She wanted to alleviate some of their anguish, move them along, at least out of her life.

That's when she saw the job advertised at Forest Lane Funeral Home and Crematorium. They were looking for a new technician to handle the cremations. A lonely job, to be sure, but helpful for her purposes.

At Forest Lane, she could spend most of her day away from the living. It made the dead seem less deafening. She had always found working in offices too loud, both the living and the expired fighting for her attention. If she let her concentration drop, she would accidentally mix the two worlds, answering the questions of the dead aloud or confusing their stories with those of her co-workers. Suffice to say, she was not very popular in the office, but you couldn't sack someone for being a bit weird. Forest Lane was different, she enjoyed opening the chapel first thing in the morning. She would often sit in one of the pews and run her hand along the smooth lustre of the wood, feeling the condensation of thought, as light and saturating as summer rain.

In the warm belly of the cremation room, Irene could give her full attention to the spirits who came to her. Most often they were those whose coffins she was handling. She would listen to their stories, then ask them if there was anything that she could do. Sometimes they just wanted to talk and Irene would settle herself at her workbench, hands clasped around her mug and listen. Sometimes they asked her to visit their stones later on. They wanted to know that they would not be forgotten, that someone would be there to care if their graves grew wild with climbers or moss. Irene became a regular at the cemetery. So much so that the groundsmen knew her by name and tended to the stones if she couldn't.

At home, Irene adopted an elderly one-eyed tabby cat that a ghost had implored her to take in. Her name was Emily, the ghost had said. "I've had her since a kitten, she won't know what to do in a shelter."

That had been a welcome request, some living company. However, sometimes the requests were too hard – relatives across the world, precise location or new name unknown. Sometimes the spirits who confided in her just didn't want to be dead; they wanted to hold their child, kiss their lover, see the world. Sometimes Irene couldn't help them, but she would cry with them.

From time to time, a ghost came to her and, like the biker at the bus stop, asked her to pass on a message. If she was lucky, it was to one of the mourners upstairs in the chapel. After the service, she would slip quietly into the crowd of well-wishers, take someone aside, and pass on the message from the spirit. It didn't always go well. Sometimes the loved one would refuse to listen, thinking her sick or mad.

Once she was even accused of being a mistress. After all, how could she possibly know all of this information about someone's deceased husband if she'd never met him before?

She recited one message only to find out with a resounding slap that it was the ghost's last passive-aggressive dig in what had been an already tumultuous marriage.

Sometimes it wasn't just the mourners who were angry; the ghosts would blame her for bad reactions, for not giving the message quite right. On those days Irene would go home with a headache after a day of scolding and berating.

Irene passed on messages and carried out errands for months, until her life was full of duties for the expired. She was tired. It was obvious that the deceased were talking her up, recommending her on some other world Yelp!. More often than not her conversations with them started with "I heard," "I was told," "There's a rumour that ..." and so forth. Soon her one-on-one conversations in the warmth of the crematorium basement turned into shouting matches, as an assembly of spooks jostled for her attention.

Not just at work, they shouted when she ate her breakfast, when she bathed, as she used the toilet, even nudging her awake from sleep to tell her to weed the stones, pen a poison letter to the new boyfriend, tell him/her/it that they loved/missed/revered/hated them. It was exhausting. She was exhausted.

Irene began to nod off at all times of the day. Her head would begin to sag as she sat at her workbench, against the tiled wall in the shower, and just before her car hit the crash barrier.

Her eyes flicked open in sudden terror as the front of the car crunched through the steel guardrail, slamming the steering column into her stomach, doubling her over like a rag doll. Her head smashed into the windscreen, leaving a mark like a spider's web. The car forged through the heavy barrier, to the edge of the bridge. She felt a sickening lurch in the pit of her stomach as it teetered, front wheels rolling desperately in thin air, and fell. The world was only pain and a kaleidoscope of air, water, and glove-box detritus before the car hit the river, hard as if it were concrete.

Frigid water rushed through cracks in the doors, windows, and windscreen, soaking Irene and wakening her to even greater pain. She gasped and gulped at the water, heavy with the taste of minerals. The car bobbed a little under the weight of water and foundered. Irene took a gulp of air before the water went over her head and the car submerged, bumping itself along the riverbed. Irene's hair rose like tendrils of seaweed in the tide, her blood blooming, swirling, and dancing in the current. She tried pulling at the doors, but they held tight with burden of the water. The last of the air was burned in her chest and her vision began to darken at the edges.

A hand curled cold fingers around her wrist. In the murky water floated a pale face, not one of rescue, but bloated and decayed, skin floating from the skull like a wedding veil. Words bubbled up from its mouth, "I heard you can help me." Beyond it floated many more, faces of the drowned snared among the riverweeds. The last of the trapped and searing air left her in a panic of bubbles and a muffled scream, allowing the river to surge into its place.

Originally published under the name Melanie Waghorne in 'Familiar Spirit' by 54°40' Orphyte Inc – 18th September 2015

LATE NIGHT BATHROOM REVERIES

A moonlit landing. One small step. To the bathroom. The sharp click of the overhead light, blinded and squinting past the mirror that shows you dishevelled and small-eyed. You wait to see if the reflection moves without you. It simply stares. The light burns your eyes, but it is a necessity. It has the power to dispel the ghostly hand that might otherwise wrap itself around the shower curtain, to turn the hulking dark figure in the corner back into the hanging towel which never fully dries. Unless, of course, you drape it over the radiator to grow crisp and rough as sandpaper on delicate, shower-reddened skin.

The light dispels all the ghouls and ghosts and boogeymen that you fear will caress the back of your ankle as you leave the dark bedroom or stroke your hand with papery grey skin and fearsomely long talons as you clasp the edge of the bathroom door. It is a small price to pay to not be alone with the demons who inhabit your house, conjured to life by your fears and anxiety and creeping, crippling dread. You wash your hands. You turn out the light and throw yourself through the bedroom door before there is a heavy step on the stairs or a shadow lurches towards you in the hall. Tucked up safely in bed, you wait for the morning light to slay all the monsters that remain.

THE HAPPIEST PLACE ON EARTH

Did you know that there is a certain theme park in the world, a park you will all know well, fronted by an iconic rodent, that seemingly has a problem with death? They claim that no-one has ever died there. But, many people, including me, know better. Their problem with the mortally challenged doesn't just stop when that person has shuffled from the mortal coil within the park's kingdom, but extends to the earthly remains of those brought back by their loved ones. A rule was put In place to prohibit any ashes being brought and scattered on the premises. Still, that doesn't stop the most industrious of mourners from sneaking the ashes of their loved ones past the turnstiles.

Obviously, you're never going to be admitted if you turn up to security with a burnished urn in your backpack. But is security always going to find a baggy of grandma's ashes stashed in your sunglasses case, or mixed into a water bottle like dead body instant mashed potatoes? No, not always. Personally, it seems a strange risk to take. If you don't lose them at the gate, you might get found out as you're dumping your surreptitious bag or bottle of remains on a ride. If they see you dumping out human remains then the ride operators will shut down the ride, escort you off, and initiate the clean-up process. Then your beloved family member, friend or lover will end up in the speciality vacuum. What will you tell anyone who asks where grandma is scattered? Funny story; she's hanging out in the vacuum bag in a phony haunted manor. Good times. Still, that might be a blessing to grandma. After all, if she's really unlucky, she might end up dumped into the water, or thrown into the background of an annoying puppet ride. Like me.

What I wouldn't give to be in the vacuum bag, emptied into a bin or chased through the park by the wind, rather than listening to this ride's cheery, upbeat but endlessly repeated song, for what I'm now terrified is…all eternity. My loved ones were smart enough, or stupid enough, depending on how you look at it, to conceal my cremains in a bottle of water each. A classic move. They brought me into the happiest place on earth and stood in line for this ride. And when the ride was dark, in between continents, my siblings leaned over the side and poured what remained of me out into the water. Discarded like the dregs of a soda you don't want to finish.

Slowly sentience returned to me and I awoke to grinning puppets in ceremonial dress, spinning wildly on their axes, the interminable bloody song blasting out of their cheerily painted mouths to drown out my cries of horror. Now I am stuck here and have been for years. And years. And years. And every fifteen minutes, the song resets itself. From when the park opens, to when it closes, every fifteen minutes of my afterlife is carved out in time and chorus and verse and bridge and melody.

I'm sure my family meant well. I am sure they did not want to damn me to an eternity of a jaunty refrain. As a family we had loved the park, returning many times, even into adulthood. There are pictures on the wall of my parents' staircase of all of us at the park, crowded into the frame in front of a ride or cramming our faces with sweet treats. The first was taken on our very first trip and we look impossibly young. That is the first picture at the bottom of the stairs as you begin to ascend. At each step we get a little older and a little bigger, until you reach the picture from the year before I died, two-thirds of the way up. I wonder if they added any more photographs after I died? To the best of my knowledge they have never returned. Or, if they have, then they have not come to this ride. I am not sure which would be worse. I look out for them every day, but I think they have abandoned me here. If I was on a rolling hilltop or neatly interred in a well-populated cemetery, maybe they'd come sit with me for a while. Tell me about their lives. But who has money to keep buying theme park tickets to commune with their dead family member?

However, I am not alone. I am not the only ghost here on this infernal ride. There are more of us than you would think. Not only those whose cremains have been smuggled in, but also those who the park's authorities would have you believe didn't ever really die here. We're dotted around the interior of the ride, skulking in the shadows or peering out from behind moving machinery to leer at the mortals riding with their mouths agape at the spectacle. Most of us are desperately trying to mind our own business. Not that it would be possible to hold a conversation during operating hours, when the song worms into your head, obliterating most cognisant thought, let alone the capacity for small talk with fellow spectres. The only one of us with some capacity is Jerry, and only because he was lucky enough to be wearing his ear defenders in the afterlife. I assume he was cremated with them. The rest of us are still in our funeral attire. Only Jerry's family seemed to have the foresight to send him on his way with trinkets required for the afterlife, like he was a Viking warrior replete with gold and furs rather than an overwhelmed millennial.

In my stiff, sombre suit that I'd only previously worn to job interviews or weddings, I watch the riders in their boats, bobbing along on jetsam-strewn water. When I have scanned the faces of all the adults and not found my family among them, I watch the children. When I first awoke, every young face was one of wonder. But as the years have gone by, the children are less and less interested in the garish, singing puppets. It is understandable that they find them less amusing these days, unlike my generation, who grew up on them, learning to count along and sound out letters in front of Sesame Street. Those that aren't bored and desperate to get off the kiddy rides are those who are more intent on the machinery, the mechanisms, the way things work. Those are the children who catch sight of us out of the corner of their eyes, a flicker that should not be there. For those children, the image of us lingers at the corners of their memory as they drift off to sleep that night, even after the excitement and sugar rush wear off.

Next time you're here, if you concentrate really hard, you might be able to see us too. If you squint into the dark spaces behind the whirling dolls, you might glimpse the whiteness of a face, the gleam of an eye or an open, screaming mouth. If you look down into the dirty water at the side of your boat, you might see the shivering sliver of one of us who has receded to the shallows to try to escape the relentless song. So why don't you do yourself a favour, make sure to write it into your will and ensure your family doesn't bring you here to join us on the spinning platforms, amongst the bright lights. It really is a small world, after all.

THE STREAK

I roll over under the covers to turn off my phone alarm, trying to not let in any cold air, and think for the millionth time that I should change the alert sound to something a little less jarring, something that sounds less like the haling of the apocalypse. Although, being awoken at any time and having to leave the warm cocoon of my duvet is always jarring, whatever tune might herald it. I check the alerts which have racked up overnight. There are a couple from food delivery and online shopping apps alerting me to deals and a group chat that I really should mute. 'It would be a shame to lose your 10-day streak' reads the notification from the language learning app I have downloaded. The alert elicits a groan. The app was downloaded in an attempt to do something a little more productive with my daily procrastination other than mindlessly doomscrolling. But, the constant notifications of the app are making me lean towards belligerence rather than enthusiasm for the task.

"You can't tell me what to do," I mutter as I clear the screen of all notifications.

If I open my phone now, I'll definitely lie in bed for at least twenty more minutes, busting for a wee and dying for a coffee while scrolling something unimportant and focus-sapping. I wish I could be one of those people who leap out of bed, maybe start the day with yoga or a cold-water swim. But I'm not. Leaving my bed is a Herculean effort that comes with more than a little moaning and groaning. The first cup of coffee is always drunk in my pyjamas. I need the caffeine before I can face having a shower or brushing my teeth. Sometimes even the coffee doesn't do it and if I have no face-to-face online meetings I stay in my pyjamas for the whole day, cup after cup of coffee making both my tongue and the surface of my teeth furry. Either way my phone is always close, faithfully waiting to be picked up and petted, like a loyal dog.

In the main, my phone is a tool that I primarily use for procrastination. I can't remember the last time I used it to make or even take a call. It is like a friend that is a bad influence, allowing me to waste an hour watching humorous cat videos or getting invested in the outcome of an argument between two total strangers on social media. With these new notifications, I don't like the turn it is taking. It is like that friend who previously encouraged you to go day drinking now dragging you along to a Bible study group or a stern teacher reprimanding you with a wagging finger from the confines of the motherboard.

I go into the phone's settings and turn off the push notifications. I'll do it when I want to, thank you very much. It is making me revert to my once teenage self who, when asked to do absolutely anything at all, even if I was just about to, would cry 'God mum I'll do it laaaaaater!'. I feel nagged by it and there is no need for that kind of negativity in my life. It is the exact reason why I do not have a partner, children, pets or any dependants at all. I want to do things in my own time and on my own terms. But the way the app is set up, the FOMO of it, the reproach of the little green cartoon bird that accompanies the notifications means I do indeed go into the app and open my lesson for the day. It will be a small victory to tick off a non-existent to-do list. I am far too disorganised to ever stick to a real one. But it does at least seem like I have achieved something today, no matter how minor.

So far, the app has taught me some weird and wonderful phrases that I don't think will really help me at all on my next holiday to the Netherlands. I'd really like to know how to ask for directions or maybe order something regular at a restaurant, like a burger or a glass of wine. I can envisage no world where I'll have to tell someone that I am an apple or that yes, I do know the duck. The latter sounds like a phrase a spy would use to ensure they are surreptitiously dropping the briefcase full of state secrets next to the right man reading his newspaper on a park bench. I know more about animals at the zoo than I do about how to order a flat white and I wonder what a waiter's face might register if I start going on about de neushoorn or de oliphant. I have not yet been taught the Dutch word for 'crazy', 'asylum' or the phrase 'please leave.'

I finish a lesson and the cartoon curser moves into the new chapter. This should be a set of lessons that will include some new vocabulary and the construction of longer sentences with a view to one day being able to carry out a conversation, rather than reciting one or two word phrases like a tame parrot. I cross my fingers that this chapter will not include any animals but thankfully it seems to be about family and houses. I guess words and finish sentences that ask me whether my sister lives with my parents or whether I live in an apartment or a house. I look around the small bedroom of my own house. I look at the velvet curtains and the art I bought myself and the fairy lights that are strung along my wall and am glad that I do not live in a house with my parents. This is all my own, carefully curated and decided by me and me alone. It is a space that I do not want to share and wish for no direction in arranging.

I never do that well in the first set of lessons of a new chapter. All the new words and phrases often throw me off because I've only just got to grips with one set before the next one starts. To try and encourage users, to make it more of a game, the app only gives you a certain number of lives at the beginning of any day and every mistake loses a one of those lives. I have only just begun but already only have one life left to use for the day. Carefully I select the right word to finish the sentence it has selected for me 'Ik hoor iets __ het huis'. I select 'onder'. Excellent! The app congratulates me and translates the full sentence – 'I hear something under the house'. The translation brings me up cold. This is not the bright daytime excursion of going to the zoo or the park or a café. It is not a sentence one might use while on holiday. It feels like a warning. Or a threat. As if coaxed to life from the app, I hear a crash from downstairs and my skin bursts into goosebumps within the warm confines of my duvet.

Closing the app, I slide out from the bed and slip my feet into my slippers, trying to be as quiet as possible. I open the phone app and dial 999, not yet pressing the call button. Keeping my thumb in place so I can connect the call at a moment's notice, I make my way downstairs to see what the noise was. I enter each room like a cop in the movies, sliding around the door jam and pouncing into the room, trying to scan all the blind spots at once. I don't have a firearm or a flashlight, just a phone tightly gripped in my increasingly sweaty hand. There are no sudden movements in my peripheral vision, no creeping footsteps behind me in the hall. There are no intruders in the house. In the living room, the curtain pole that I was so proud of putting up on my own is swinging loose from one end, like a sleeping arm falling out of bed. The loose end has cleared a nearby shelf of its collection of knick-knacks. That must have been the noise I heard.

The empty window, devoid of its normal dressing of heavy curtains, draws my eye, like a missing tooth in a bright smile. The early morning world beyond it is still dark, its contents blinkered from me by the glare of the overhead light. Anyone could be looking in at me. Or anything. Shuddering slightly, I turn off the light and retreat to the kitchen, to the cosiness of pulled down blinds and the waiting coffee machine. There is no way I can deal with either a clean-up or impromptu DIY without the aid of caffeine first.

My work day is longer than expected, involving more painfully explicit explanations to coworkers than usual. By the time I log off I am both mentally and physically exhausted and doing DIY seems a torturous concept. Instead, I take my laptop to bed and vegetate under the duvet until it is time to go to sleep. I put my phone in its normal place and turn out the light. It feels as though I have barely been asleep when the alarm wakes me. I roll over and paw at the phone but it is not in its usual place. Groaning I turn on the bedside lamp and look for it. It is not on my bedside table, it is not on the floor. I can't see it anywhere. But I can hear it and the sound it is making is not the normal alarm sound that I keep reminding myself to change. Instead it is something discordant, out of tune and time. It grates on the inside of my skulls like ragged nails. Eventually I drop to my knees and feel around, like a cartoon character who has lost their glasses and definitely can not see without their glasses. Finally, my fingers touch the cold surface of the rapidly vibrating screen. It is just underneath the bed.

Whipping the phone out from under the bed I tap the screen. It is only an hour since I went to sleep and the sound the phone is making is definitely not my alarm. The icon on the lock screen is of the little green bird from the language app. And he looks mad. 'IT WOULD BE A SHAME TO LOSE YOUR STREAK' the notification says, all in caps, taking up the majority of the screen. I have never seen this before. Getting back into bed, I turn out the bedside lamp and open the phone. Clicking the notification is unavoidable so the app opens immediately after I key in my passcode. It bathes my face in the sickly green of the app's background, bringing light to all the corners of the room.

Instead of opening to my progress page like normal, it automatically begins a new lesson. The first question is the same one as yesterday, asking me to complete the statement 'I hear something under the house'. The sentence is even creepier to see in the middle of the night. I click 'continue' at the bottom of the screen. The next question has the computer-generated voice speaking a sentence and asks me to translate. My finger trembles as I select all of the words to create 'I hear something outside of the house'. I'm so tense and my ears are straining so hard that I counsel myself the scraping noise I can hear is merely a branch hitting the roof or a vehicle in the distance. I click continue. I don't want to understand the next sentence. But I do. I hear something inside the house. Ik hoor iets in het huis.

"Inside the house", I whisper to myself. In het huis.

I hear the curtainless window downstairs open, the click of the latch as it releases. I hear the noise from outside as the window yawns open to let in whatever it is that has decided to commune with me through this device. An electrical séance.

I drop the phone onto the covers and the sickly green light bounces off the ceiling, skidding across the wall as the phone slides down the covers, over my knees brought up to protect myself. It settles on the door of my bedroom. There is a tread on the stair. There is the breathy brush of something along the wall of the hallway. 'Mag ik binnenkomen?' flashes up on my abandoned screen. A weight on the handle of the door. 'Mag ik?', the phone presses. Questioning. Searching. 'Ik kom binnen' appears on the screen. I am coming in. With a sob I grab the phone and click out of the app, holding my fingers down on the power button until the phone shuts off, casting the room back into the darkness of the night outside, hoping that will be enough to stop the questions, the statements from inside.

The door opens. I can hear the squeak of its hinges. I throw myself from the bed, launching my entire weight against the door. But it is too late. The door does not close all the way. There is something wedged into the gap between the door and the wall. The papery crisp leather of an unknown hand, gently, lightly brushes against my own. I scream. And scream and scream. A sound that does not need to be translated, a sound that makes sense in any language.

A DAY IN THE PARK

The ghost felt the weight of life in that place as keenly as a knife blade pressed to the tender flesh of a throat. The brimming fullness of it was a slap in the face of their demise that could not be escaped. It was bad enough when the park was closed, when all they had to contend with was the sound of the earthworms moving through the ground or the whisper-thin touch of an insect as its feet kissed a leaf before taking off to freedom, to somewhere other than this place. The gentle sweep of leaves through the air on a warm breeze made them want to scream, to clutch at their head and block it out.

The park was at its very worst when it was full. When the grass was trampled with screaming, laughing, vibrant children or the air buzzed with the scolding of frazzled parents who had just noticed the well begged for ice-cream dripping down freshly washed clothes. That was when the visitors' vitality accentuated the stopped clock-ness of the ghost's new existence.

The ghost preferred it when it rained, when all they had to contend with were hardened dog walkers whose charges insisted on going out, even in the middle of an icy downpour. When sulking children looking glumly out of rain-slicked car windows were taken home to complete homework or to blankly watch cartoons they had seen before.

But even in the rain, even in the dark, the ghost was never truly alone in that place. There was another here. Just a little scrap of mist, barely there and yet still unable to move on from the mortal place. Painfully unformed, the little scrap had not had a chance to develop fully in life and in death had become a small patch of mist flecked with pain and heavy with the strong smell of spun sugar on a hot day. The ghost had been there when the child had choked. They had watched the father frantically pounding the child's thin back as he had desperately struggled for air around that spun nest of sugar. The ghost had watched as the child turned, casting vaguely accusatory, confused eyes to his shrieking mother. Those eyes. Those eyes had seemed to ask her why she could not fix what was wrong, like she had a thousand times before, in the kiss of a skinned knee or in soothing whispers whispered after a particularly bad nightmare. Why could she do nothing about the half-chewed wad of pearly pink candyfloss that had been so begged for and was now wedged too far down his throat to be retrieved but was too sticky to be swallowed. Why?

The ghost had watched the terrible events unfold Without being able to do anything at all but watch. They had stood beneath the tallest tree in the park and felt the blue and red lights pulsing through them when the emergency services arrived, to no avail. They had watched until every single person left the park and the small patch of mist had reconstituted, hovering over the grass, still-flattened from their prone body. The ghost had been vaguely annoyed at the little scrap, this unseen, unknown potential of a person who was now haunting the same space. The sight of them was both a reminder and an accusation.

The ghost had kept to the other side of the park from the scrap, not wanting to feel the hint, even the suggestion of a small hand pushing into their own. They did not think they could bear that. So instead, feeling like a coward, they had hidden from the little mist, eyeing it through the rough squares of the playground cargo net or through the dancing leaves from the shedding bushes by the picnic benches. Why did it have to be their problem? Coping with their own pain was bad enough, without taking on that of another too. It wasn't fair, the ghost thought, inwardly cringing at their own churlishness, at the whine that resonated through their own mind. Not fair. Not fair. Not fair. Shan't. Shan't. Shan't. So there.

The little scrap made no effort to move towards the ghost. It simply floated around the space where it had happened, where their knees had buckled and their little face had pressed into the sun-warmed grass to stare unseeing at a ladybird picking its way delicately up a blade of grass before opening iridescent wings to take flight to somewhere unknown. *Ladybird, ladybird fly away home. Your house is on fire and your children are gone.* Only a part of the nursery rhyme forming before fizzling away as synapses fired their last.

The parents came and laid flowers in the spot. They were always something red or white or yellow, something far too jolly and bright for the occasion. The little scrap watched them as they did so. They came every year, holding on to one another like they might break apart, white fingers pressed into the flesh of bare arms else they be washed away without the anchor of each other's bodies. The ghost could not stand the sound of their sobs as they placed the fresh cut stems onto the earth. But one year they returned and the mother's hands were not pressed into the solid arms of the father, or hugging her own thin frame. That year the mother's hands clasped a small scrap of impossibly soft fabric with a red, angry face peeking out from within. Another little scrap to have chafed knees kissed and bad dreams soothed, to grow and form and become more than a permanent toddler.

The little mist did not make a sound at their approach but the ghost could feel their sadness all the way across the park, weighing them both down like rain trapped within a storm cloud. The ghost thought they could see the mist momentarily darken although it could have been a trick of the light, the sun moving behind a cloud, the day ticking closer to dusk. The swaddled baby's cry was a cleaver ripping through the quiet of the park and sending its parents scurrying away from that place to burp or bounce or change or soothe it. A younger sibling always hungrily taking attention away from an older brother who they would soon overtake in age and would never know.

The ghost watched the parents leave. They waited until the park returned to bird song and whistling wind before they moved across the space. They stood next to the little scrap and gathered it close to them, feeling the mingling of their vapours as the little scrap leaned into them. The ghost imagined the feeling of a hot, little hand, sneaking into their own.

DR CADAVER, MD

Colin

Colin knew that the results could not be good when he received the phone call from the hospital on Monday morning. The secretary who called to make him an appointment with a consultant was far too sympathetic and the appointment far too swift. He knew better than to ask what she knew. He wasn't sure he really wanted to know the answer just yet anyway; let denial be a balm for a little bit longer.

The receptionist who checked him in at the front desk had the same overly-sympathetic tone as she told him to take a seat. Colin thought there was a very real possibility that he might throw up on her shoes. He was glad his wife wasn't with him to witness that. He wanted to spare her the worry until he knew there was something to really worry about.

He'd always assumed it was a cliché used by ham-fisted television producers when a ringing sound was used during a scene of a character receiving bad news, scoffing when watching the same tired trope again and again. He now realised it was simply a depiction of the truth. The words coming out of the consultant's mouth were oddly muffled as a hot wave of nausea coursed through Colin's body, making him feel sick from his stomach to his toes. Every nerve and muscle felt oddly tensed, as though each separate part of him had slept funny and awoken from a nightmare tingly with pins and needles. He wondered if the diseased cells that had taken up fierce residence in his organs felt the same; maybe they were belligerent and unmoved, or in a celebratory mood, having heard they were about to win.

He didn't trust himself to drive home and left his car in the car park, wandering down to the bus stop to stare unseeing at the neon display counting down the minutes till the next bus arrived. The disappearing numbers made him even more nauseous and oddly hysterical, a display of vanishing time that seemed to mock him and his condition personally. He had sat on the cold, uncomfortable bench and laughed until tears dripped into the corners of his mouth, a contorted comedy and tragedy mask of a face that scared away everyone else waiting for the bus. The driver seemed unmoved. How many people had he driven away from this stop outside the hospital on the very worst day of their lives? How many people did it take to make such a sight boring, samey, pedestrian even? Colin didn't want to think about it. He sat in the priority seating at the front of the bus and cried for the entire journey. He cried again the next day when he returned for his car and saw bill for a twenty-four-hour stay in hospital parking.

The visit to his GP this morning had been far less emotional and far more clerical. The amount of administrative work that came with dying surprised him. Sitting across from the doctor, a man who knew Colin's body intimately and whose first name Colin could not even remember, he signed the forms that would promise his disease-riddled body to science on the conclusion of his life. Since his diagnosis, so many decisions and choices had been taken away from him. It felt good to actually make at least one plan of his own. Donating his body had not been his original plan, but after seeing the package prices of funerals in his local undertakers, a shock that almost hastened Colin's advancing demise, it had seemed a good one. What a waste it had been to scrimp and save for the majority of his adult life, if he couldn't even afford a decent box in which to be lowered into the ground. The paperwork had assured Colin that after his body was used to teach young medical professionals, it would then be cremated at the hospital's expense. Done and dusted, his final dispatch would be someone else's problem, which suited Colin down to the ground. Or perhaps into the ground, he thought darkly. Who knew death would give him such a gallows sense of humour!

As he stepped out into the cold air from the stifling heat of the GP surgery, his name signed on the dotted line, Colin took a deep breath. He let the air settle in his chest, thought about the oxygen permeating his cells and blood, and then let it go. He imagined letting go of more than the held, de-oxygenated blood. It was the calmest he had felt in weeks. Colin waited for regret to set in, to second guess himself, but the decision remained sound in his mind. A fine idea, practical and even, he thought to himself with a touch of smugness, even a little altruistic – giving something back to the medical community, even if it was his old, spent body. Even amidst the flurry of appointments, last ditch treatments, palliative care and more, he felt no misgivings.

However, Colin found that he was rapidly regretting that decision when his ghost stood over his own cold, grey cadaver in the chilly clinical classroom in the bowels of the hospital. His face was covered by a draped sheet but he was mortified to see that his genitals had not been afforded the same dignity. The smell, he assumed, of formaldehyde was strong in the air. It smelt sharp and tangy, like the hospital had hosted a BBQ and a thousand pickle jars had been opened and smashed in an orgy of vinegary celebration. His body was shrunken and grey, pumped full of the fixatives needed to keep him from putrefying on the metal gurney before the students could learn all they could from his insides.

The sensation of looking down on his prone body was vertiginous. He might have swooned, like a Victorian debutante, had he the body required to complete the action. To Colin, he looked like a life-sized jelly baby and not even one of the good flavours. Nobody would willingly choose the grey baby! That wouldn't be anyone's favourite! Everyone knew the yellow ones were the best, he thought. At the idea of his favourite confection, Colin expected his mouth to water, but nothing happened. Clanking his jaws together, he found that the motion was still possible, but saliva, like sweat, blood and other fluids, had been drained out of him before his mandatory attendance at this gross anatomy class. The thought of saliva was now a figment of his non-corporeal imagination. What else was now a ghost's pipe dream? Rumination threatened to overwhelm him. He had to concentrate.

Turning back to his prone body, he walked or

floated (who could be sure of the exact mechanism!) around it, peering at it from angles that would not have been possible in life. He inspected the leathery soles of his feet, the right turning in slightly, a pigeon toed stance that he had always worked hard to conceal, the left with the beginning of a bunion on the edge of his long, hairy big toe. Spider veins raced up his calves and disappeared behind his knees, the right one the culprit in ending a promising football career. He avoided looking too long as his crotch. It was cold down here, plus he was dead. There was no shame, but he desperately wanted to cover the sad little creature. He went to cover it with his hand but his new ghost limb disappeared through his grey skin and into the metal table beneath, pitching him forward. He stood quickly, the chemical, pickly smell now a taste in his mouth. Had he managed to taste his own skin? Yeuch!

Colin stifled a scream when the laboratory tech charged with making sure all the bodies were ready before the first class walked through him. It was frigidly cold already in the room, but both the tech and Colin shivered violently at the contact. The tech tasted like old oil from a deep-fat fryer, burnt and dirty with a film of leftover crispy offerings. Colin wondered about the state of his arteries. He'd been so preoccupied with himself and his return that he had not noticed the other man in the room, but he was enormously grateful when the tech gently laid a cloth over his groin. With both his face and crotch covered, Colin's body was rendered almost anonymous and, without the distraction of his face and naughty bits, Colin was able to pay attention to the rest of his body. He tried to ignore the discoloured bruises from IV ports and injections on the backs of his hands and in the crooks of his elbows. Instead, he concentrated on the strong muscles of his biceps, that had once twirled his wife around a packed dance floor, the once hard muscles of his stomach that had softened with good food and too much beer and the chest that he had sung from with full force while listening to the radio in the too-hot kitchen, cooking the good food that had made him soft. There was a great swelling of love for that body. It seeped around his embarrassment and mingled with the sadness that he no longer inhabited it.

Nostalgia threatened to overcome him. He felt the urge to crawl back into himself, lie in the dark cold space, nestled against dead spleen and liver and un-beating heart, and go to sleep, but from the corridor came a great cacophony of noise – the students were here. Colin could hear them outside the classroom's doors, some of their voices too loud, tinged with the nervousness of being about to see their first dead body. Colin was sure that learning about the body in a classroom was very different from picking up a scalpel and pushing it into once living flesh. As they spilled into the cold room, rubbing their arms and exclaiming over the chill, Colin was aghast at how young they all looked. Had he really entreated his body to a bunch of children? They'd probably laugh at him, call him names, exclaim over his wobbly bits. He tried to steady himself. Everyone looking so young was surely just a by-product of his age. These were the doctors of the future. They were duty bound to take care over him, surely? Especially with their teacher watching. Still, he didn't want to see what was about to happen. He imagined a sharp flash of steel pressed into his sternum, sliding down his chest and belly, the flesh peeled back like something consumable. How had he come to be here? There had been no bright light and no long tunnel. He had just awoken and climbed out of his dead skin like a caterpillar sloughing off a chrysalis. He wasn't at peace. Instead, he was pissed off and embarrassed and confused. Religion hadn't been that prevalent in his life but he would be lying if he hadn't hoped, just a little bit, that once he left the ravages of his sick body he'd float up onto a cloud and it would be all rainbows and angels with harps and saints playing drafts. He hadn't expected that the first thing he would see after shuffling off this mortal coil would be his own sad, shrivelled penis. The indignity!

Wrenching his eyes away from that miserable organ, Colin wondered why was there no-one else here? Why was he the only ghost forced to watch this? There weren't ghosts from the rest of these bodies crowded around, inspecting their own vessels like tourists in a museum. What had he done that was so egregious that he had to put up with this torture?!

Pushing himself into the furthest corner of the room, Colin watched as three of the students were allocated his body. They read his stats from a laminated sheet at the end of the gurney on which he lay – his age, his gender, his cause of death, and other pertinent facts. Was that all he boiled down to? It was barely a paragraph. Those details did nothing to encapsulate the entirety of his life. It was not a fitting eulogy. Colin wondered if he'd been rash to do this, if it would not have been kinder to let his friends and family have a proper funeral for him no matter how cheaply they'd had to do it, a symbolic dirt to dirt followed by a brow' buffet of dry crinkled sandwiches and lacklustre pastry. Had his family done anything at all to commemorate him? Or, once he had shuffled off the mortal coil, had they simply taken the plastic bag of belongings offered to them by a nurse and gone home to watch the telly and make themselves dinner? How cruel it seemed to wake up here rather than back at home, listening to the sounds of his wife moving around the hallway in her slippers, flipping the switch of the kettle, humming along to the radio – all the sounds he had heard while sick and prostrate in their marital bed before departing for hospital to eke out his last breaths in an unfamiliar bed. What a comfort that would be, rather than the chattering of strangers and the clang of metal trolleys and sterile equipment in this cold, unknown place.

The students allocated to his body stood around it, looking down. Two boys and a girl. If he could, Colin would have blushed deeply at these kids with their taut young skin looking down at the saggy ravages of his own. The first two were cocky, joking and jostling with each other over the materials given out by their tutor. Colin disliked them already. The third was quiet, casting furtive glances at Colin's naked body. Colin didn't know if he was an introvert, nervous or just overwhelmed at being effectively given a corpse: Colin's corpse. The boy was slim, with dark eyes and dark floppy hair that he continually pushed behind his ears, even though it kept falling back into his face. *He needs a haircut*, thought Colin. *Who knows what is going to end up on his hand? He can't keep wiping it through his hair.* Paternally, he wished he could smooth it away from the boy's face and get a proper look at him. His wife and he had not been blessed with children. They had tried for many years, to no avail. In their day, it wasn't something you went to the doctor about; it was something private that either happened or didn't. They had loved each other fiercely, but Colin often saw the flash of pain in Sylvia's eyes when their friends brought round mucky little bundles for her to coo over. Who was with her now? Was she alone? Did she have people around her? Colin longed to see her again. Maybe this was just an aberration, and if he tried really hard he could get back to her.

Colin squeezed his eyes tight and tried to imagine her face. The last time he had seen it, she had been leaning in to kiss him for the final time. He had felt the hot droplets of her tears slide down his cheeks as she leaned in. No. He didn't want to think of her like that. He tried to remember her on the dance floor during the first dance at their wedding, her face flushed with champagne and embarrassment at being the object of everyone's stares. If only he could step back into that memory. He tried, but it didn't work. Behind his closed eyes, he could still hear the chatter from the students and feel the chill of the classroom. He squeezed them as tightly as they would go. The tendons of his neck strained, as did his biceps, triceps, and all the small muscles of his hands until his nails dug into the inside of his fists. But nothing happened. He strained hard, hoping that ghosts weren't able to shit their pants because, if they could, he was certainly playing a dangerous game. Nothing. He was stuck.

Opening his eyes again, he turned away from his body with a snort of frustration and scanned the classroom instead. Each group were poring over the details of their charges; he tried looking over their shoulders at their new pet cadavers but the sight of so many dead bodies was making him anxious, even though he was dead himself. The room was small, full of the living and the dead. Skirting around them he inspected the rest of the room – a desk, a door, not even any windows. He tried to lift papers from the tutor's desk. Not even a flutter. He inspected the door. There was no way he could open it himself, but he'd been able to pass through things already. Taking a short run up, Colin launched himself at the door. His mouth filled with the taste of pencil shavings, musty and cloying. He felt the denseness of the wood all around his ethereal body. Just as he felt he was about to be crushed by the weight of wood around him, he was spat back into the classroom. He could go no further. Trapped. Shit. Picking himself up from the floor, he moved back to his body and began to watch the lecture. There was simply nothing else to be done. Only to watch. And wait.

<u>Steven</u>

Of course, Steven had known that studying to be a doctor would eventually involve the dissection of a human being. He'd been in classes for weeks studying every aspect of the body, seeing structures within cadavers blown large on the screen in the lecture theatre. However, a slide with zoomed in graphics was very different to being presented with a real live, or recently live, human being. Like a lot of his course, the theory was proving very different to the reality.

He hadn't been able to sleep the night before. He was so nervous that every time he closed his eyes he saw the slides from his lectures. Swimming under his lids were the diagrams of the brachial plexus, the median, ulnar and radial nerves. In the dark of his dorm room Steven extended his own arm into the blackness, feeling the muscles tighten. He felt his own sinews and nerves react to the messages sent from his brain, felt his fingers curl, the nails digging into the soft flesh of his palm. Into the darkness his whispered the five components of the brachial plexus – roots, trunks, divisions, cords, and branches.

Next, he stuck his leg out of the covers, feeling goosebumps jump out on the flesh of his thigh. He thought about the femoral nerve, the iliacus muscles and hip flexors. Why count sheep when you could count the myriad of connective tissues that made up the human body? He had never been so acutely, painfully aware of his own body before. Every movement made a word pop into his mind, as effervescent as bubbles in soda. He felt the sheet against his skin – *epidermis*. A spot began to itch on his cheek – *buccal*. Maybe he needed to urinate? – *cystis*.

Eventually the sun's rays began to peek out from beneath the curtain, their tendrils reaching across the carpet to tickle his closed lids – *blepharal*. Slowly, he pulled himself upright and lowered his feet to the floor. *The thigh bone connected to the hip bone. The hip bone connected to the back bone. The back bone connected to the shoulder bone.* The catchy song playing incessantly in his head was not much better than the deluge of medical terms. He found himself humming the tune at breakfast, walking down the corridors, even in the locker room putting on his scrubs and apron outside of the gross anatomy room.

He followed his peers into the classroom and felt the chill of the refrigerated air on his tired face. It was like walking out into the middle of a snowstorm with only thin scrubs as protection, but it did something to wake him up. In front of him were several metal gurneys with a bucket hanging at the foot of each one. On top of each gurney lay a cadaver. All the spittle in Steven's mouth dried up. Even though the class had been scheduled for late afternoon, several hours after lunch, Steven still felt his undigested egg salad sandwich make a mutinous roll in his stomach. He belched gently into the back of his hand, letting the slightly eggy cloud mingle with the scent of the formaldehyde in the air. It was not an appetizing mixture and he thought he may well be skipping dinner that evening.

The bodies dotted around the room didn't quite look real, more like props in a movie. Was it because their faces were covered or was it the strange hue to their skin? Or was it because he had watched too many horror movies in his teens? He half expected the still forms to pull away their own shrouds and swing stiff legs over the edge of the gurney to plop down onto the cold lino below, dead limbs dragging across the floor as they advanced on him. Soon he would be expected to cut into one of these people. What an odd thing. No-one he knew, barring his tutors, had ever cut into a body before. Well, as far as he was aware. Maybe the postman, his mum's old neighbour or his high school science teacher, were secret serial killers, sawing into limbs in their quiet suburban basements. His lunch quivered again and sweat jumped out on his forehead, rapidly cooling to a thin sheen in the frigid air conditioning.

What was he going to say when his mother called him this evening to ask how his day was? He imagined recounting the class in intimate detail to her and hearing her retch, heavy and full into the mouthpiece. This wasn't normal. Why couldn't he have wanted to be a gym instructor or a civil servant instead? He certainly wouldn't have been facing years of schooling and debt ahead of him, and there would have been fewer dead bodies! Hopefully, at least. He'd have to be a pretty poor gym instructor to be faced with a corpse in that line of work. Nervous laughter bubbled behind his ribs. He swallowed it down like acid reflux.

The tutor stood gravely in the middle of the room, a stamen surrounded by corpse petals, and gestured to their new charges.

"These people are your first patients. They have given up their bodies so you can learn. They can no longer experience pain but that doesn't mean that you don't owe them your empathy. They must be treated with the utmost respect. These people are going to help you to become the best doctors you can be."

The mood in the room was grave and Steven took longer than was necessary reading the scant details of his cadaver from the laminated sheet. He'd been so preoccupied with thoughts of himself that he hadn't even considered what these people had done, what they had gone through or the lives they had lived. He felt more than a little guilty having previously imagined them as the walking dead from some Hollywood movie. He smoothed the hair down behind his ears, a nervous gesture he'd had since childhood. His mother had been so annoyed with it in his youth that she'd made sure his hair was always kept short. She'd relaxed her conditions somewhat when he'd went to secondary school and he'd grown it out. The nervous tic had resumed almost without his knowing it. The latex smell from his glove wafted into his nose, a pleasant reprieve from the formaldehyde, as he pulled the strand back behind his ear. He'd have to consciously remember to not do it once the dissection began.

In the first instance his tutor had them turn the body on to its front. Steven now understood the term "dead weight". The body was an unyielding slab of meat that required the help of both of his classmates to manoeuvre. Steven felt the cold of the cadaver seep through the thin material of his scrubs as he used his body weight to brace against its shoulder. Huffing and puffing, the three of them managed to turn Colin's body, exposing the long muscles of the neck, shoulders and back. They spent some time pointing out different thoracis and cervicis muscles, obliques and the lumbar triangle. Steven began to forget that this was a person. It was simply another exercise to be completed and knowledge to be consumed. As the session went on, he became more and more comfortable handling the frigid flesh. He was surprised, when his tutor called an end to the session, that none of them had yet to even hold a scalpel.

"Today was about getting you comfortable. The next session we will begin the dissection."

For all his former consternation, Steven found he was disappointed to not be going further. He hoped that meant he was simply excited to learn and not some kind of weirdo. He was the last student out of the room. Making sure the rest of his cohort had left, Steven returned to his body. He placed his hand against its shoulder – *scapula* – and patted the unmoving flesh.

"Thank you," he whispered to Colin's face under his shroud.

If only he had known or could see, in the dark recesses of the classroom's corner, a ghost fighting back tears that no longer existed.

<u>Colin</u>

Colin didn't know how long he had waited in the gross anatomy lab. After the class had dispersed, their footsteps receding behind the door he couldn't pass through, he had waited. Even with the door open he hadn't been able to venture into the corridor beyond. The air through the open door was thick and viscous, barring his way. It felt better than being stuck in the door's woody interior. But not by much. Dejected, he stood in the middle of the classroom, unsure what to do with himself. He felt like a friendless child left behind at playtime, with no-one to notice. Soon, the technician returned to tidy up whatever the students had missed. He wore oversized earphones and the tinny beats of his music leaked into the room, like a distant party that Colin hadn't been invited to. There hadn't been many celebrations in Colin's recent history, but he found that if he screwed his eyes up tight and really concentrated, he could remember a couple.

He was surprised to find that the first that came to mind was his nephew's first birthday party. His wife had stayed up most of the night to make a cake that the child would only be interested in sticking his fat little fingers into, but even so, she spent hours getting it just right. All the family had crushed themselves into his brother's small dining room, extolling the baby's cuteness – round cheeks under a jolly party hat, the elastic cutting into his chubby chin. Colin remembered the jaunty music and his wife trying to hold back the tears that this tableau would not be repeated in their own future. His voice had cracked on the first verse of Happy Birthday.

Searching for a happier memory, Colin cast his mind back to their wedding day. He could remember how nervous he had been beforehand, his clammy hands failing miserably to tie his tie, before his best man had stood in, knotting it tight against his Adam's apple. The ceremony itself was a blur, but he could remember their first dance, the smiling faces as they twirled around. If he tried really hard, he could almost remember the words from the song that had been playing the night they first met. A jukebox in a long-forgotten pub. All ghost notes from the past now.

"HELLO!" Colin shouted at the technician. "CAN YOU HEAR ME?" he hollered, like a reverse séance.

The man did not react. Colin tried waving his arms in front of him, an aircraft marshal of the dead, hot-stepping to avoid bodily contact and the consequent horrific tasting of yet another human. No reaction. Colin didn't know if it was the man's headphones or his own new state of being, but it seemed like he could not communicate with the living. Whether this was permanent or not remained to be seen. Maybe if it was something he could practice. The technician switched off the lights before leaving, plunging the classroom into darkness. Colin was alone once more.

He didn't know if he slept or if the lack of energy in the room had put him into a state of inertia but Colin was only aware of himself again, unaware of how long he'd been on his own, when the fluorescent lighting blinked back on. A stifled yelp rang out from his lips into the chilly air, like a kicked dog. The student's conversations as they returned were loud, but their enthusiasm infused him with energy. He didn't even mind when his body came back out of cold storage. It was like coming face to face with an old friend. Learning what today's lesson would consist of dulled his enthusiasm somewhat. The purpose of the students' first class was mainly to familiarise themselves with a cadaver. Today they would be cutting into them. Colin had the heebie jeebies but tried to console himself with gentle self-interrogation and logic – *What did you think was going to happen when you gave them your body? Of course they were going to cut into you.* Maybe being here was lucky. He could have woken at a body farm, gently decomposing in a field with no-one to talk to, no sound but the wind whistling through his exposed ribcage or a critter gnawing on an uncovered, stripped femur. He could have woken beside his body in the cold, dark earth.

Colin had spent so long ruminating on what could have happened to his body that he'd missed what was actually happening to it. The group assigned to him worked together to turn him, straining and trying not to laugh at each other's puffed cheeks and tensed muscles. Colin tried not to be offended. He hadn't been the most svelte of men, but he didn't think he was three-people-struggling heavy. Carefully, they let his arms dangle down from the edges of the table and propped blocks underneath his chest. The tutor helped them place the blocks, telling them this was to keep the muscles tense, so they'd be better able to visualise them. Colin felt nervous, like a case of stage fright, hoping his body was going to be able to perform, to live up to its intended duty. Once in place, the group stood around his prone frame, taking a moment to assess the enormity of what was about to occur. Colin watched as Steven's arm extended, hand reaching for the dissection instruments.

Steven was so intent on the scalpel, a sharp slash of steel illuminated under the fluorescent lights, that his hand was beginning to shake, almost imperceptibly to anyone but Colin who was staring just as hard at the instrument. He held his breath along with Steven and they both gently exhaled when scalpel met flesh, the slight bounce of treated skin before it split open like overripe fruit. Colin saw the tremor in Steven's hand at the force needed to slice through skin and muscle and fascia, saw the way his own body opened up like a terrible flower in bloom. Without the flow of blood, the structures were clearly visible and shockingly vivid – like a Goya painting. Both men stood back, looking in awe at the body in front of them.

"Come on, slowpoke," whispered Steven's classmate impatiently. The class had a list of structures to identify, and he was desperate to get to his turn. He held his hand out for the scalpel.

Colin bristled on Steven's behalf. Why couldn't the lad get half a chance to compose himself? It was a shock. He himself was shocked and he was dead! Without thinking of the consequences, Colin gave the over-eager classmate a shove in the middle of the chest. Instead of passing through the boy's flesh, his hand made contact with his sternum. It wasn't much of a shove, more a fleeting moment of contact, but the boy still took a surprised step backwards, confusion registering on his face, his hand dropping to his side. Colin could taste his confusion, something fizzy and bitter, like soda water. It leached the ire out of him, leaving him as blinking and confused as Steven's classmate.

Such was Colin's confusion at this new change in his being that he barely watched the rest of the dissection. He spent the rest of the class testing out his boundaries – shuffling towards the concrete wall of the classroom and feeling the coldness seeping into his palm as he laid his hand across it. He didn't go through. Colin decided to try the doorway again, bracing himself for the discombobulating sensation of being within and part of an inanimate object. His touch lighted against the metal handle and did not go through. Colin exalted, a cry of success like watching your favourite team score the winning goal. He might not have gone through and into, but that didn't mean his spectral body had gained the strength to turn the handle. It simply lay on top, like a cold, dead fish. He had to stop himself from jumping up and down with joy that he wouldn't be left passive and helpless, that even now, dead and alone, something had given him back a touch of agency. Baby steps, he told himself, trying to temper the flush of joy, not wanting to get ahead of himself.

"Thank you, son," he said to Steven, clapping a hand onto his shoulder, feeling the heat of him through his shirt.

It warmed something in Colin's core, radiating out to his limbs, like coming into a warm room from out of the cold. His hand did not pass through, but Steven's terror, his anxiety and concern did. It tasted to Colin like gasoline and burnt hair. He wished he could give some of the warmth back, drip in his paternalistic feeling, his pride and protectiveness. Baby steps. He had time to learn. He had nothing else in the world but time.

At the end of the class, the door into the corridor was opened and students began to depart. As a group stood around comparing notes, Colin decided to try again. He sidled up to the open door, hoping another invisible barrier wouldn't stop him, but he passed through easily out into the corridor, which smelt like dust balls and floor cleaner. Freedom! The corridor took him to the students' locker room, which smelt even worse – formaldehyde scented scrubs, body odour and feet. To Colin it was a fine perfume, the smell of changed circumstances. He inspected every inch of the room, marvelling at every detail. When he had inspected every nook and cranny, he decided to look into the lockers. It felt voyeuristic. Shame prickled at Colin. But who was going to know? How could any student know a ghost had been poking around in their belongings?

There was no way he'd be able to open any of the doors by himself, and he didn't want to get trapped in anything again. He wondered if he came at a structure with enough force whether he would be able to pass through? After several attempts, his mouth cold and tasting metallic from his exertions, Colin managed to shove his head into the first locker. It smelt strongly of perfume, vanilla and sandalwood notes in the enclosed space of the locker. The back of the door was covered in glossy photographs, a slight girl he had noticed in the classroom standing victorious on top of a high mountain, sweat beading her forehead as she raised her arms in triumph. There were professional photographs from a prom, candid snaps with friends and more formal set ups with what Colin assumed were family members. He exited the locker and thrust his face into the next. And like this, Colin passed a very pleasant afternoon, viewing and tasting and smelling. He found old socks, older sandwiches, lucky charms, annotated texts, photographs and keepsakes. He revelled in the lives of the students to whom he had entrusted himself, hoping to forget that his own life was very much over.

When every life had been pored over, so thoroughly that Colin now thought of them as fondly as old friends, he got to wondering about Steven. Did he live in halls of residence? Was he at his desk now, studying, or out with his friends? Colin was curious about the life the custodian of his body was leading. He decided to find out.

Steven

Steven felt overwhelmed. His head swam with all the terms, names and archaic Latin prefixes and suffixes he'd recently learnt. They would not get straight in his head – haem or hemi, phleb or phren. They danced in front of his eyes like pink elephants, as elusive to pin down as hallucinations. Steven closed his eyes, squeezing them shut to concentrate, but behind his lids was only the image of his cadaver, flayed open on the bench, yellow fat and spongy empty veins, like something from a true crime documentary. His stomach churned uneasily, full of acid and very little else. He hadn't been able to face eating any dinner. Again. Every time he brought anything up close to his mouth, he caught the whiff of formaldehyde and, whether that was in his imagination or not, he simply could not stomach putting the morsel into his mouth. All it made him think of was rot, of death and blood and guts and gore. His hands were raw from scrubbing, but the phantom scent still clung to them. How on earth was he going to be a doctor if the dissection of a cadaver affected him so badly?

The thought of dropping out of this coveted (and very expensive!) course only made his stomach churn harder. He had worked so hard to get here, and every member of his family was so proud of him. The weight of their expectations pressed heavily on his shoulders, forcing his body into a prone position over his textbook, his muscles beginning to cramp from lack of movement. Steven rubbed his face and closed the book. Nothing more was going to lodge in his brain tonight. Opening the bottom drawer of his desk, Steven stared at the long, taupe book within. The sketchbook hadn't made it out of the drawer once since he'd started medical school. There had been no time for hobbies. The very thought had seemed frivolous and vaguely ridiculous.

He'd been a talented artist in school, always doodling on the side of his assignments and positively glowing with enthusiasm in every art class. All of his other subjects required his brain to be working hard, engaged, heavy and dense with effort. To Steven, art was a way of letting go, of disengaging, letting his imagination take over, almost a therapeutic act. He could let his hand and brain run away together, like lovers eloping. There was no room for that here.

Pulling the sketchbook out now, he flipped back the heavy card cover and ran his palm over the pristine first page. The paper was rich, thick and brimming with possibilities. His heart rate began to slow, soothed by the familiarity of the sensation under his hand. Beneath the book was a tin of fresh pencils. The smell as he opened the case was evocative, bringing a smile to his tired face. Steven took the first pencil out of the box and laid the nib against the page. It reminded him of holding the scalpel earlier in the day. The pressure of the pencil pushed against points on his fingers made sore by his scalpel; he hadn't realised how similar his grip was. Out of both instruments, the pencil felt more natural. Less destructive. With the pencil he could create, whereas wielding the scalpel felt like he was destroying his cadaver, one slice at a time. He had not yet considered that the scalpel would soon be an instrument to fix what was broken, to return to a patient a life back that was dangling in the balance.

Steven began gently sketching Colin's form from memory - the bulk of his shoulders, the shape of his trunk, ending just above his buttocks. He let the pencil flow over the paper, judging the length of the arms, the positioning of the neck. The thought of Colin's body became more palatable, a life drawing model rather than a prop from a scary movie. Soon the outline of Colin was solid on the paper, almost as real as when Steven had looked down on him with anxiety earlier in the day. Steven started to fill in the detail at the top of Colin's back. First, he sketched in the Trapezius, accurately rendering the triangular shape of the muscle, from the back of Colin's neck over the upper part of his shoulders. In his mind, he heard his tutor's voice telling him how to place it in relation to the seventh cervical and dorsal vertebrae. Once done, Steven labelled the muscle in his cramped hand. Next, he drew the Latissimus Dorsi in the lumbar region, just above the pelvis in the lower part of Colin's back. He labelled this too. From there, the terms almost tripped off the end of his pencil, layer by layer – the Rhomboideus minor and major, Serratus posticus superior and inferior, down to the level of the spinae. Steven's hand positively danced across the page, turning Colin's prone body into anatomical art on the paper. A smile crept across his face. He hadn't felt this kind of confidence in weeks.

As though the smile, the warmth of confidence, had jinxed him, Steven's hand stopped, dangling above the paper. The name of the last section of muscles had escaped him. He scoured reams of information in his head but could not alight on the correct term. The precise anatomical name evaded him at every turn, darting down the labyrinth of his synapses like a hunted animal. A fat tear of frustration plopped onto the paper, smudging the annotation for the Piriformis. He put his hands over his sore eyes, gritty from too much concentration and not enough sleep. If he could have only seen the ghost at his side, heard the reassuring words of a man impressed with his skill and heartsore that he could not help further, it might have stayed his hand. Instead, he reached out, placing his palm flat on the paper, and flexed, thinking about how the flexor digitorum superficialis was contracting, how the metacarpophalangeal joints were working in creating the fist that crumpled the thick piece of paper into a ball before lobbing it into the bin.

If Steven had not slept so heavily, woken so late and had to rush around his room, brushing his teeth while pulling on socks, he might have seen the attempt someone had made at smoothing the badly-creased paper in his trash can.

Colin

The paper had been the first thing Colin had managed to exert any influence over. And even then, it had not been much. He had not been able to grip it, only use his palms in an attempt to smooth its crumpled surface. His hand had passed through more often than not, coating his mouth with the gluey sensation of chewed paper, but he'd had to try. Steven was a beautiful artist and Colin couldn't bear to see all that talent, all that effort, or, maybe even a little selfishly, his own body be simply tossed away out of frustration.

Why now? Colin wondered. Was it simply because he had been around for longer, or had the act of the students cutting into his body that day released something? Made him grow stronger? It didn't really matter. There would be no answers, so what was the point in even asking the questions? That thought stopped him in his tracks. He would have to learn to let things go, not obsess over them, continuously worrying at them until they were threadbare. His wife had bought him *'Zen and The Art of Motorcycle Maintenance'* one year for Christmas, but he couldn't get on with its philosophical nature. It had sat unfinished in the living room bookcase. Maybe death would make a philosopher out of him yet!

After doing the best he could with the drawing, he turned to look at Steven, who was snoring gently in his bed. Watching the boy sleep, seeing his face grow younger as it relaxed into unconsciousness, made Colin wonder if this is what fatherhood would have felt like. He hoped he would have been the kind of parent who'd have watched his child sleep and felt a tender part inside ache for his troubles. Surely, he would have been the sort of dad to see his child's artwork lying in the bin and try to fix it, to make it better? He hoped he would have been, but there was no telling. Maybe he would have been a father quick to anger, burnt out from lack of sleep, from working hard to support his family. He was not able to give his wife a child, but maybe he could give this child a father figure?

Around dawn Colin started wandering the halls, hearing the rest of the students snuffle and snore in their beds, before returning to the place where his body was stored. He climbed in next to his cadaver, and even though he wasn't tired, not in the same way as when he'd been alive, he tried to get some rest of his own.

A squawk jumped from his lips when his drawer was roughly opened and his body pulled out into the bright fluorescent lights of the classroom. He might not sleep anymore, but he had experienced something approximating a dozing state. He had dreamed, watching excerpts from his life flit past him, faster and faster, as though he was riding a carousel which had gone rogue, being battered by a centrifugal force of memory and regret in a kaleidoscope of colours and faces. Leaving that place was a relief. If his heart hadn't been removed, he was sure it would be pounding a crashing crescendo in his chest right about now.

He watched the lesson with enthusiasm, finding that if he pretended that it was not him on the slab, then the class itself was very interesting. He'd always enjoyed learning, although admittedly not so much in school where every fact was learnt by rote and parroted back. But, as an adult, he had enjoyed ploughing through the non-fiction section of his local library and had bored his poor wife to tears with his preference for documentaries over any kind of entertainment show. He had read the newspaper religiously and devoured any pamphlet he came across, be it in the waiting room of the dentist, doctor or optician. Without the stressors of everyday life – there were no chores when you were a ghost, no need to do the washing up, take out the bins, wash, shave or even find a change of clothes – he could stand alongside this cohort of students and absorb every word their teacher told them. So, he decided that was exactly what he was going to do.

Walking around the campus, in and out of classrooms, dorms and lecture theatres had ceased to be a problem. But Colin was unable to go outside or leave the grounds. He had tried several times. It was almost as though something knew, could peer into his ghostly brain and see his plans. If it was a short walk outside across campus, he could will himself to the other building with ease. One moment he was in one building, the next in another, but he seemed to have no ability to be outside. If he stood in a building and thought about the road he could see, travelling away from the school, somehow making it home, he became stuck. Sometimes for the rest of the day, left to wander the building he had found himself in, unable to escape to another. Thinking about the outside world, the spring breeze, or the solidity of pavement rather than scuffed linoleum under his feet rendered the rest of his day useless. If only he could leave, see his wife again, run his hand over her cheek, then maybe he could move on. But he couldn't. Like the first day, the day he had awoken in the cold classroom, he was still totally, inexplicably stuck. His leash was longer, but he was still tethered.

So, for several years, Colin sat beside Steven during lectures, seminars and demonstrations. He was surprisingly good for an old man, and even better for a dead man. Sometimes, when Steven was particularly stuck, Colin would lean over and breathe the answer into the cornice of Steven's ear. It was probably wishful thinking, but, more often than not, Steven sat up straighter in his chair, his eyes brighter and the answer on his lips. Colin swelled with paternalistic pride. Steven's confidence had grown and grown. He slept better, panicked less and his sketchbook filled with one anatomical drawing after another. His skills increased in both his chosen fields. Colin wished he could tell him how proud he was. Sometimes he spoke the words as he watched over Steven at night, hoping they, like his lecture hall answers, would seep into Steven's unconscious and take root there.

Colin watched with a tear in his eye when the group of students assigned to his cadaver finished their gross anatomy studies and his post-mortem services was no longer needed. He had hoped that his wife, any of his family, might attend the cremation of his remains, but he overheard the lecturer informing Steven and the others that his wife had declined to attend and that his ashes would be sent to her directly. His body ached to see her again, but as that now seemed unlikely, he had hoped that the final burning of his earthly remains might be the catalyst to shift him fully from his mortal coil. All the while he watched his body burn in the cremator, he hoped to experience some change, some lightness taking over him, dispersing him like an early morning mist to whatever was next. Instead, he watched his mortal body break down, crumbling to lumpy grey matter, sieved and tipped into a utilitarian urn. Would he be sitting in that urn on the mantel over their fireplace? What if she didn't live in their old home anymore? Maybe she had found the house too big, too unmanageable, selling it to live in some unknown bungalow he would never see. The thought threatened to uproot him. There was change all around him, lives progressing, evolving, and Colin was in no position to hold on. He was to be swept away like his ashes.

Graduation was fast approaching. Colin had heard all about it as he eavesdropped on the students. What if they all put on their cloaks and took their paperwork and disappeared, and Colin was left behind? Like an old piece of furniture no longer wanted or needed. He'd grown attached to Steven, watched him flourish into a capable young man who, Colin thought, would have an exemplary career as a doctor. Colin could not bear the thought of Steven packing up his room and going out into the world without him. Everyone he cared about was out in the world without him, moving forwards. He could not bear to be left behind.

As Colin watched Steven pack up his room, the weight of unshed tears pressed behind his eyes. He had no idea if a ghost could cry. He moved around the room behind Steven, watching him place his belongings in boxes and bags, panic began to move through his form like static electricity. He was desperate. Colin took a deep breath, held it tight and walked into Steven's receding back, hoping with all of his might that he would not just pass through the young man and be forced to watch him leave for the last time. Instead of passing through Colin felt himself flatten, sliding over Steven's back, down his arms and across his shoulders like syrup, clinging on to his form. He felt warm and liquid, heating up with Steven's body temperature, absorbing some of Steven's anxiety to be leaving, his excitement at this next challenge, his youth and vigour. The feeling of dissipation, of amalgamation made Colin want to scream, to pull himself apart atom by atom. But he remained, clamped down tight over the skin of his charge.

As soon as Steven had made it down the stairs and sat heavily in the back of his parents' car, Colin disentangled himself from his body and slid into the seat next to him, like a puddle of melted snow. It took a while for him to come back to himself, folding and melding until he became the shape of the person he had been once again.

Steven

Steven was glad to be finished with medical school. He was looking forward to being placed in his first internship, practising medicine in a real hospital. He hadn't realised how badly he had wanted to leave school until his last day. As he hoisted the last box of his belongings up into his arms a sensation came over him, a cloak of overwhelming sadness settling heavily over his shoulders. It was a struggle to lift his feet from the utilitarian dormitory carpet and begin the descent down to his parents, who had agreed to help him transport his belongings. Steven felt old before his time, his body ached, and a feeling like loss seeped into his very centre, making his face throb with unshed emotion.

Sliding himself into the back of his parents' car, he

leaned his face against the cool pane of glass and looked up at the building he had spent years living in. It was the first place he had lived since his childhood bedroom. The first place that really felt like his own, that he had organised and decorated a little to his own tastes, and was his own responsibility. Maybe that was where the feeling of loss originated, maybe that was all adulthood was, a succession of tiny losses growing greater and greater, accumulating over time. As he watched the town creep past the car's window, he felt some of that sadness leach from his body, overrun by a budding nervous excitement about what the future might hold for him now. He was standing on a precipice, ready to take the big jump into the rest of his life.

Steven was pleased with the hospital in which he had been assigned his internship. For one it wasn't far from his home; some of his classmates had been saddled with hellish commutes, some even having to move away altogether. The hospital in which Steven found himself, in what still felt like the middle of the night, on his first day was one he remembered from childhood, some hazy memory of an X-ray after a particularly egregious tackle on the school sports field, his mother apologising for Steven tracking mud through the corridors from the bottom of his boots to a technician who could not have cared less.

Now he was no longer accessing the building as a civilian, no longer relegated to a moulded plastic chair to wait his turn, watching doctors and nurses move with unknown purpose through the corridors. Now he was one of those doctors, permitted to view the inner workings, behind the scenes of the place. Steven was thrilled. Even if the first of those inner sanctums was the staff locker room, with its mildewy smell and vending machine that would contain more than a few of his future cobbled-together dinners.

Of course, Steven was nervous that he would now be treating actual patients, that their lives were effectively in his hands. But every time he started to flounder, he would think of his old cadaver, trying to visualise whatever body part was causing his patient's ailment. Whether he imagined the preserved internal structure of the body itself or the drawing he had made that evening to solidify that knowledge, he found it helped ground him, to calm the fierce beating of his heart and allow the knowledge he had accrued through all his schooling to come to the fore, rather than letting his nerves get the better of him. Steven had learnt to trust his intuition, his gut, almost as though his guardian angel were whispering the answers to him as he stood over a person possibly undergoing the worst day of their lives.

Because of his stoic nature, Steven's attending physician recommended that he consider specialising in emergency medicine. He had told Steven that he'd watched his interactions with patients and been impressed with his bedside manner. He'd advised Steven that they needed people who were able to keep their cool, work methodically and without panic in intense situations whilst always keeping patients at the forefront of whatever they were doing. Steven agreed and chose it as his speciality. He had come to enjoy the variety that came from working in the department, never knowing what patient might come through triage to be presented in the bay, or whisked through the double doors on a gurney from the ambulance. No two days were ever the same.

Colin

Following Steven out to the car from his school, and his first day at the hospital, were the only times Colin had tried to piggyback his ghost self onto a living person. The process was too painful, too unnerving and strangely intimate for him to try with anyone else. He felt guilty enough trying it on Steven, but he wanted to be there for the boy, there to give him some comfort on what might be an overwhelming first day. Colin had grown accustomed to the medical school. He'd found the experience so interesting that there was no way he was going to be left behind on Steven's first day at the hospital.

After Steven had made his way into the staff locker room to change into his scrubs, Colin slithered from his body, pooling under one of the locker room's benches to wait until his form coagulated back into that of a ghost. A second successful piggybacking completed. He stuck close to Steven for the entirety of his first shift, observing his somewhat shaky interactions with his first patients, hearing the slight tremor in Steven's voice as he introduced himself and began asking questions of them. Colin stood beside him, quietly murmuring his support to the young man in low, soothing tones. He told him to take a breath, to think about everything he had learned. After spending his entire afterlife at the school, Colin found he could impart some of the knowledge he had accrued there, whispering to Steven to check a patient's airway first or alerting him to the monitors registering a downward trajectory during the chaos of a fraught situation.

After Steven's first shift, Colin decided to stay in the hospital. If he returned home with Steven, he would only have to keep piggybacking onto him to travel back and forth. Colin could not face it. So instead he watched Steven change out of his scrubs in the locker room, walk down the corridor and make his way to the car park from a window in the ward. Colin spent the rest of the night moving between wards and departments, marking time until he could see Steven again.

For the most part Colin liked the hospital. There was always something going on, even very late at night. If he needed quiet, he could retreat to one of the wards, dozing in the dim light from the nurse's station, lulled by their low voices. Or, he would join the new babies, tightly swaddled in their bassinets in the nursery, before one would rouse him with a piercing shriek. If he needed a bit of action, to feel part of the world again, he could take himself down to the emergency department. Perusing the selection in the waiting room, Colin would select a patient, something interesting, not a broken bone or someone in need of stitches after a messy Friday night but someone that required diagnosis, and would stick close to their side. He enjoyed watching the diagnostic process from start to finish. He tried to internalise the knowledge he was amassing from these interactions, hoping he could use it to assist Steven as he progressed in his career.

Colin was following a young man, who, in his opinion, had presented with a classic case of gallstones. He stood next to the man's head as the doctor performed the ultrasound, observing the ghostly forms with acoustic shadowing in the man's gall bladder. He listened to the man's history, nodding sombrely as he explained it was not his first attack and agreeing with the clinician when he advised that due to repeat attacks it was probably better to have the organ removed.

"Cholecystectomy," Colin said with confidence, only a beat before the doctor uttered the same word.

He was getting good at this. Colin had watched Steven grow, go through his internship, his residency, watched him take on interns of his own and impart what he thought of as their combined knowledge to his students. Colin was surprised at the depth of his own knowledge after so many years shadowing both Steven and the other doctors in the hospital. He considered this as he followed the patient's trolley down the labyrinthine corridors to the surgical ward where the man would wait until his planned surgery the next day. Colin was busy thinking about the stages of a cholecystectomy. He thought about the patient being sedated, his abdomen inflated for better visualisation and the four small incisions required for a laparoscopic procedure. As he began to envisage the retraction of the liver, Colin was suddenly assaulted by a scent.

It curled around him, as thin and fine as mist but as strong as a coiled rope holding him in place. It was not one of the usual smells of the hospital, to which he was well attuned, antiseptic and alcohol rub, but the smell of something much more familiar. The smell was his wife's perfume. The same perfume she had spritzed on her delicate throat and the pale insides of her wrists on the day of their wedding and every day since then. It was the scent he'd breathed in on their pillow cases, as she'd walked past him in the morning, as she'd leant over his shoulder to place a cup of coffee before him, as she'd bent to kiss him. But it wasn't just the perfume, it was the scent of her hair, the smell of her skin, the essence of Sylvia all around him in this sterile corridor.

Moving down the corridor as fast as he could, drawn by the fragrance as surely as a bloodhound, Colin chanted her name. She was here. He was sure of it. Rounding the last bend he came to the geriatric ward. Quietly he moved to the bed at the end of the room, slipping between the curtains which were not fully drawn. In the twilight of the room Colin saw the diminutive figure of his wife in the bed. She was so frail. He was shocked at how old she had become now their roles were reversed, standing over her hospital bed as she had stood over his, watching the slight rise of her chest under the scratchy sheets.

The bay was full of her smell, but under it there was something else, something sickly, tinged with disinfectant and sour breath. Why was there no-one with her? No friend or comforting presence to hold her hand. Colin looked wildly around but there were only the other patients in their beds, the soft murmur of voices from the nursing station. Colin sat at his wife's side, tasted the moulded plastic on his tongue as it came into contact with his form. Gently he hovered his hand above her own, felt the slight warmth from her skin as she slept. Colin stayed in place for the rest of the night, listening to her breathe and watching her eyes move rapidly under their lavender lids. He hoped she was dreaming something pleasant, maybe of him, of them together.

In the morning, Colin was heartened to see Steven round the corner onto the ward. He was a fine young man, Colin thought, looking the right amount of imposing and assured in his white coat, the plastic snake of a stethoscope around his neck. It wasn't unusual for Steven to come to the wards to see what had happened with a patient he had treated in accident and emergency. In Colin's opinion it was one of the things that made Steven such a good doctor. The ghost had seen many doctors during his tenure in the hospital's halls, and especially in the emergency department, who didn't even know their patient's name, who talked about them just the other side of the blue curtains as though they weren't even there. The best doctors made sure to learn the patient's name, looked down into their faces, placed a calm, warm hand on their arm or leg and told them that they were there to help. That they saw them. Colin especially knew how important it was to be seen.

Steven was one of those doctors. He was coming to check in on Sylvia even though she was no longer one of his patients. As much as Colin appreciated it, he hoped that Steven would also guard his heart, not burn himself out on the suffering on others. He watched as Steven studied her chart.

"Keep her comfortable", Steven told the nurse as he passed back her chart. "It probably won't be long now. Any family?" he asked.

The nurse shook her head and Colin returned the gesture. She did have family. He was there. Holding his breath, Colin slid onto the bed next to Sylvia, just as he had climbed into bed next to her a thousand times before when he was alive. But this time she didn't turn to him, half asleep and partly opening her eyes in his direction for him to plant a kiss on her upturned face. Colin knew that Sylvia was never going to open her eyes again. He had been in the hospital long enough to read the cues on the doctors' faces, especially Steven's. He could read Steven's face like a poker player. Steven's tell was a crinkling in the corner of his left eye, the beginning of a wink that was barely noticeable to anyone not looking out for such a movement.

Pressing himself against her body, Colin felt her skin beginning to cool – it would not be long. As he had once done to Steven, Colin piggybacked onto his wife's body, flattening his own form across the well-recognised curves and planes of his wife's figure. He tried to breathe in the smell of her, tried to ignore the acrid taste of her sickness in the back of his throat. Liquid, he pooled around the curve of her jaw, into the hollow of her neck and down her arms, trying to give her some comfort, to hug her to him with everything he had. Colin felt her slowing heartbeat and tried to match his breath to it, their bodies humming together, slower and slower. Colin heard her last breath. Held his own, waiting to hear her next shallow rattling gasp through the pain of his liquidity. It didn't come.

Nothing happened.

Colin waited. Waited for something to happen. Anything. Would his wife awake as a ghost, like he had? How long had that taken anyway? Would the porters come, take both of them down to the mortuary, to the cold, dark drawers to await collection by the funeral home? Would she wake at all? Colin wondered if there was going to be a bright light, was he going to watch Sylvia's soul exit the husk of her body and carry on to the afterlife without him? Would she know he was there with her? Colin wasn't sure how much longer he could wait, how much longer he could maintain his shrouded form as a protective layer over his wife. But the thought of standing up again, of being apart from her and alone again was more painful than his quaking atoms.

Slowly, warmth began to flood through him. It wasn't Sylvia's body; he could still feel the chill of it beneath him but he was starting to warm. Holding on with all he was worth, Colin knew this was what he had been waiting for. Sylvia's essence had begun to leach from her skin, squeezing through each pore, bonding with him. At last Sylvia was with him, entwined and entangled; they warmed and gelled and pooled together. At the end of all things for both of them they were finally reunited. Colin felt his essence coming apart and coming together with her, becoming more and less at the same time. Colin turned his last conscious thought towards the boy, now a man, who had taught him so much. As he and his wife turned to vapour together, dissipating in the gathering dawn of a morning neither of them would see, Colin thanked Steven. And said goodbye.

ABOUT THE AUTHOR

Melanie Atkinson is a UK horror author living on the south coast with her husband and dog. She can often be found penning horrible little stories in her vegetable garden with a large cup of tea.

Other Titles:

The Last Night In Amsterdam
The Woods Are Full of Eels
Work? Shmurk!